*Agnes*

# *Agnes*

by Peter Stamm

*translated from the German*
by Michael Hofmann

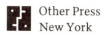

Other Press
New York

Copyright © 1998 by Peter Stamm

Originally published in German as *Agnes* in 1998 by
Arche Verlag AG, Zurich-Hamburg

Translation copyright © 2000 by Michael Hofmann

First published in English in 2000
by Bloomsbury Publishing, London, United Kingdom

Poetry excerpt on page 123 from "A Refusal to Mourn the Death,
by Fire, of a Child in London," by Dylan Thomas, from *The Poems of
Dylan Thomas*, copyright © 1945 by The Trustees for the Copyrights
of Dylan Thomas. Reprinted by permission of New Directions
Publishing Corp.

Production editor: Yvonne E. Cárdenas
Text designer: Julie Fry
This book was set in Quiosco with Aries by
Alpha Design & Composition of Pittsfield, NH

10 9 8 7 6 5 4 3 2 1

Library of Congress Cataloging-in-Publication Data

Names: Stamm, Peter, 1963– author. | Hofmann, Michael, 1957
    August 25– translator.
Title: Agnes / Peter Stamm ; translated by Michael Hofmann.
Other titles: Agnes. English
Description: New York : Other Press, 2016. | Description based on
    print version record and CIP data provided by publisher; resource
    not viewed.
Identifiers: LCCN 2016020726 (print) | LCCN 2016008316 (ebook) |
    ISBN 9781590518120 (ebook) | ISBN 9781590518113 (hardback)
Subjects: LCSH: Storytelling—Fiction. | Man-woman relationships—
    Fiction. | Psychological fiction. | BISAC: FICTION /
    Contemporary Women. | FICTION / Literary. | FICTION /
    Psychological.
Classification: LCC PT2681.T3234 (print) | LCC PT2681.T3234 A7313
    2016 (ebook) | DDC 833/.92—dc23
LC record available at https://lccn.loc.gov/2016020726

Publisher's note: This is a work of fiction. Names, characters, places,
and incidents either are the product of the author's imagination or
are used fictitiously, and any resemblance to actual persons, living or
dead, events, or locales is entirely coincidental.

*St Agnes! Ah! it is St Agnes' Eve —*
*Yet men will murder upon holy days.*

—John Keats

# 1

Agnes is dead. Killed by a story. All that's left of her now is this story. It begins on that day, nine months ago, when we first met in the Chicago Public Library. It was cold when we first met. It generally is cold in this city. But it's colder now, and it's snowing. The snow is blowing across Lake Michigan, on the gale-force wind I can hear even through the soundproof glass in my picture windows. It's snowing, but the snow won't settle, it gets picked up and whirled on its way, and only settles where the wind can't get at it. I've switched off the light, and look out at the illuminated tips of the skyscrapers, at the American flag that gets tugged this way and that by the wind, in the beam of a searchlight, and at the empty streets far below, where, even now, in the middle of the night, the lights change from green to red and red to green, as though nothing had happened, or was happening.

This is where we lived together for a while, Agnes and I, in this apartment. It was our home, though now that Agnes has gone, the place seems strange to me, and impossible. Agnes is just a step away, no more than a thickness of glass, but the windows don't open.

For about the millionth time, I'm watching the video that Agnes made of the day we went hiking—on Columbus Day. *Columbus Day in Hoosier National Forest*, it says, on the box and the cassette, in her tidy script, underlined twice with a ruler, like the way we used to underline the answers to our math problems when we were children. I've got the sound switched off. The pictures seem so much more real than this darkened apartment. They have a peculiar radiance, the radiance of a great expanse of open country, on an October afternoon.

An empty expanse, no town for miles around, no village, not even a farmhouse. Staccato shots, without much variety. A series of fresh starts, attempts to capture the landscape. Sometimes I am able to guess what prompted Agnes to press the record button: a peculiar-shaped cloud, a billboard, a strip of forest in the distance, hard to make out through the wide-angle lens. Once, there's a pan across to me, driving. I make a face. And then she tries to film herself filming, I suppose: the rearview mirror, and the camera looking into it, and Agnes, barely discernible, behind it. Then once, very briefly, Agnes, driving this time, holding her hand in the way.

The park ranger. He too puts his hand in the way, but unlike Agnes, he does it laughingly. A zoom down to his hands, which are smoothing down a map, pointing to a track that doesn't show up in the picture. The ranger falls back in his chair, opens a drawer, and pulls out various brochures. He laughs, and holds one up to the camera: *How to survive Hoosier National Forest*. The image wobbles, and then a hand comes up into shot to take the leaflet. The ranger is speaking all the time, his expression getting more and more serious. The camera turns away from him, and brushes by me on its way. Suddenly there's forest, a little stand of trees. I'm lying on my back, asleep, perhaps, or just with my eyes shut. The camera moves lower and closer until the picture goes fuzzy, then it pulls back. Then it pans down to my feet, then up to my head again. It stays on my face for a long time, moves in again, but the picture blurs again, and it pulls back.

"No videos?" the guy in the shop with the slicked-back hair asked me when I went down for a six-pack a couple of hours ago. He asked after Agnes. She's gone, I said, and he smirked back at me.

"They all go," he said, "don't worry, there's lots of pretty women in the world."

Agnes never liked the guy in the shop, though she couldn't give a reason why. She just said she was scared of him, and when I laughed at her, she laughed as well. She was scared of him, the way she was scared of windows that didn't open, or of the droning of the air conditioner at night, or the window cleaners balancing on their platform outside our bedroom window one afternoon. She didn't like the apartment, the building, or even downtown. At first we laughed about it, then she didn't talk about it anymore. But I realized her fear was still there, it had gotten so big she couldn't talk about it anymore. Instead, the more frightened she got, the more she clung to me. To me, of all people.

# 2

I was sitting in the Public Library, leafing through bound volumes of the *Chicago Tribune*, as I'd been doing for days, when I first saw Agnes. It was last April. She took a seat opposite me in the big reading room, probably by chance, because it was pretty full. She had a little foam-rubber cushion with her. On the table in front of her, she laid out a pile of textbooks and a writing pad, two or three pencils, an eraser, and a pocket calculator. When I looked up from my work, our eyes met. She looked down, opened the first of her books, and started reading. I tried to read the titles of her books. She seemed to notice, and pulled them nearer, with the spines facing her.

I was working on a book about American luxury trains, and was just reading about the political debate on whether the army should be called in during the Pullman Strike. I'd gotten rather bogged down in this strike; it wasn't relevant to my book, I was just fascinated by it. In the course of my work, I've always let myself be guided by curiosity, and in this case it had taken me miles away from my subject.

From when Agnes sat down opposite me, I hadn't been able to concentrate. She wasn't that striking-looking, slim and not very tall, brown hair thick and down to her shoulders, a pale complexion and no makeup. Only her eyes had something unusual about them, an expressiveness I haven't often seen.

I couldn't claim it was love at first sight, but she interested me and took up my thoughts. I kept looking across at her, it was embarrassing almost, but I couldn't help it. She didn't respond, never looking up once, but I'm sure she sensed she was being looked at. Finally, she got up and went out. She left her things spread out on the table, and only took her calculator with her. I went out after her, not really knowing why. When I got to the entrance hall, there was no sign of her. I walked out of the building, and sat down on the stairs to smoke a cigarette. It wasn't cold, but I was shivering anyway, after sitting around for hours in the overheated library. It was four in the afternoon, and the people on the sidewalks were a mixture of tourists and shoppers and a few early office workers.

There was already an intimation of the desolate evening that lay ahead of me. I hardly knew anyone in this city. No one at all, actually. Once or twice I'd fantasized about women's faces, but I knew enough not to pursue those sorts of feelings; I'd only get hurt. I had several failed relationships behind me, and for the time being, without having come to any sort of conscious decision about it, I was reconciled to being on my own. Even so, I knew I wouldn't be able to get on with my work as long as that girl was sitting opposite me, so I decided I'd go home.

I stubbed out my cigarette and was just about to get up when she sat down on the steps no more than three feet away from me, with some coffee in a paper cup. She'd spilled a bit of it, and she set the cup down on the stone step, and wiped her fingers with a crumpled tissue. Then she took a pack of cigarettes from her little rucksack, and started fumbling for some matches or a cigarette lighter. I asked her if I might give her a light. She turned to me as though in surprise, but I saw no surprise in her eyes, only something I didn't understand.

"Yes, please," she said.

I lit her cigarette for her and another one for myself, and we sat and smoked for a while, not speaking, but half facing each other. Eventually I asked some trivial question, and we started a conversation, about the library, the city, the weather. It wasn't till she got up that I asked her what her name was. She said she was called Agnes.

"Agnes," I said, "that's an unusual name."

"You're not the first person to say that."

We went back inside the reading room. Our little conversation had released my tension, and I was able to work again, without having to keep looking across at her. When I did, she looked back at me with a friendly expression, though not smiling. I stayed longer than I'd meant to, and when Agnes finally packed up her things, I asked her in a whisper whether she'd be here again tomorrow.

"Yes," she whispered back, and for the first time she smiled.

# 3

I was back in the library early the next morning, and even though I was waiting for Agnes, I had no trouble concentrating on my work. I knew she would come, and that we would talk and smoke and drink coffee together. In my head, our relationship was already much further advanced than it was in reality. I was already wonder-ing about her, beginning to have my doubts, though we hadn't even been out together.

I was working well, reading and making notes. When Agnes arrived, around noon, she nodded to me. Once again, she put her foam-rubber cushion down on a chair near me, spread out her things as she had done yester-day, picked up a book and started reading. After about an hour, she took her cigarettes out of her rucksack, glanced down at them and then across to me. We both stood up and walked, either side of the broad table, toward the passage in the middle of the room. I accompanied her to the coffee machine, once again she spilled some of her coffee, once again we sat down on the library steps. The day before, Agnes had seemed rather shy; now she spoke quickly and hurriedly, which surprised me, as we were talking about trivial subjects. She was restless, but even so—knowing no more of one another than our names—we seemed to have become more intimate overnight.

Agnes talked about a friend of hers called Herbert, I can't remember how we got onto him. Herbert had recently had a strange experience. Agnes told me how he was having a drink in the bar of a big hotel. It was afternoon.

"I've been there a couple of times with him myself," said Agnes, "they have a piano player and the best cappuccinos in town. A short flight of steps leads down from the lobby into the café, past an ornamental fountain, and just as Herbert was going down the steps, there was this woman going the other way. She was about the same age as him, and was wearing a black dress. When he saw the woman, Herbert says, he had this strange feeling. Like a mixture of sadness and belonging. He felt as though he knew her. But he was quite certain he'd never seen her before. At any rate, he felt overcome by weakness, and just stood where he was."

Agnes put out her cigarette on the step, and dropped the end in her empty coffee cup.

"The woman stopped as well," she went on. "For a few seconds, the two of them stood facing each other. Then the woman slowly walked up to Herbert. When she was standing right in front of him, she raised both hands, laid them on his shoulders, and kissed him on the mouth. Herbert says he tried to put his arms around her, but she pushed him away and took a step back. Herbert stood aside, and the woman smiled at him and carried on up the steps. As she walked past him, she brushed his arm with her hand."

"Strange story," I said. "Did he try and find out who she was?"

"No," said Agnes, and as though suddenly embarrassed that she'd told me the story, she got up and said she had to get back to work.

The following day, when we met for the third time, I asked Agnes if she felt like going to the coffee shop opposite.

"They bring you the coffee there," I said, "so you won't get your hands all dirty."

We crossed the road. Agnes insisted on using the pedestrian crossing, and waiting for the *Walk* sign at the lights.

That coffee shop was where I'd been having my coffee almost every morning for weeks, and reading the paper. It was a bit run-down, and the red leatherette benches were yielding and unpleasantly low. The coffee was thin and often tasted bitter from standing around on the hot plate for too long, but I liked the place, because none of the waitresses knew me or talked to me, because I didn't have a special place where I always sat, and because someone asked me every morning for my order, though it was always the same.

I asked Agnes what she was working on. She said she'd studied physics, and was working on her dissertation. It was on the symmetries of crystal structures. She had a part-time assistantship at the Mathematical Institute at Chicago University. She was twenty-five.

She said she played the cello, and liked painting and poetry. She'd grown up in Chicago. Her father had taken early retirement a few years ago, and her parents had gone to live in Florida, leaving her here on her own. She lived in a studio apartment in a suburb. Agnes didn't have many friends, just three women who played in a string quartet with her that met every week.

"I'm not a very sociable person," she said.

I told Agnes I wrote. She took no notice, didn't ask me any questions about my work, and I didn't mention that I'd had books published. I was pleased about her lack of interest really. I'm not particularly proud of having written nonfiction, and there are more interesting things to talk about than cigars, the history of the bicycle, and the luxury train.

We talked about ourselves only briefly; instead we discussed art and politics, the coming presidential elections in the fall, and the responsibilities of science. Agnes preferred a general or abstract conversation about ideas, even later on, when we knew each other better. Her private life didn't engage her much at the time, or at least she didn't talk about it. When we discussed things, she spoke very earnestly, and she had strong opinions. We spent a long time in the coffee shop. We didn't leave until lunchtime, when the place started filling up, and the waitress got impatient with us.

# 4

For a few days, we only met in the library, and didn't arrange to see each other outside. We often smoked our cigarettes or drank our coffee together on the steps, and slowly we got used to each other, the way you might get used to a new garment that you hang up in the closet for a long time before daring to put it on. Finally, after a couple of weeks, I asked Agnes to dinner. We decided to go to a little Chinese restaurant near the university.

When I got to the restaurant that evening, there was a woman lying on the sidewalk outside. She wasn't moving. I knelt down beside her, and gave her a cautious nudge. She was no older than Agnes. She had red hair, and her skin was pale and freckled. She was wearing a short skirt and a dark green sweater. She didn't seem to be breathing, and I couldn't feel her heart when I put my hand under her sweater. I rang the emergency number from a telephone on the corner. The woman on the other end asked me for my name, address, and telephone number, before finally agreeing to send an ambulance.

"Is the person dead?" she asked.

"I don't know. I'm not an expert," I said. "I imagine so."

When I got back to the restaurant, a little knot of passersby had collected around the girl, and we waited in silence for the ambulance to come. It arrived five minutes later, just as Agnes was walking down the street. She had been at a rehearsal for her quartet, and was carrying her cello.

I talked to the paramedics, told them it was me who had found her, as though it was something to be proud of.

"Dead," said the driver. "She's made it."

Agnes stood next to me, waiting. She didn't ask me any questions, not then, nor over dinner. She sat very erect, ate slowly and carefully, as though needing to concentrate so that she didn't make any mistakes. As she chewed, she displayed the tension of a musician waiting for her next cue. Only once she'd swallowed her mouthful did her face relax, and she seemed relieved.

"I never cook for myself," I said, "just easy, quick things like scrambled eggs. I like cooking for other people. I tend to eat much more when I'm in company."

"I don't like eating, period," said Agnes.

I had coffee after dinner. Agnes ordered tea. We'd been sitting in silence for a moment when she suddenly said: "I'm afraid of death."

"Why?" I asked in surprise. "Are you sick?"

"No, I don't think so," she said, "but everybody has to die sometime."

"I thought you were being serious."

"I was being serious."

"I don't think that woman suffered much," I said, to comfort her.

"I wasn't talking about her suffering or not suffering. As long as you suffer, you're at least alive. It's not dying I'm afraid of, it's death. Just because that's the end of everything."

Agnes stared across the room, as though she'd spotted someone she knew, but when I turned and looked, there were only empty tables.

"You don't know when it's the end," I said, and, when she failed to reply: "I always imagined it was like feeling tired and lying down, and being able to have a rest at last."

"You obviously haven't thought about it very hard," she said rather coldly.

"No," I admitted, "there are other things I'm more interested in."

"What if you die sooner?" she said. "Before you feel tired, if you don't need a rest?"

"I won't be ready to die for a long time," I said.

We didn't talk. I tried to think of the words of a Robert Frost poem, but they wouldn't come. I paid the bill, and we left.

It seemed inevitable that Agnes would come back with me. I live on the twenty-seventh floor of the Doral Plaza, a high-rise apartment building in the downtown area. In the lobby, we ran into the guy in the shop, who was just locking up. He winked at me, and smirked. "No videos tonight," he said, and sighed deeply and pleasurably. I ignored him, and just walked past.

"Who was that?" Agnes asked in the elevator.

I took her hand and kissed it, and then we kissed in the elevator until it stopped with a little ping on the twenty-seventh floor.

# 5

Everything happened very quickly. We kissed in the corridor, and then in my living room. Agnes said she had never slept with a man, but when we went into the bedroom, she was very calm, took off all her clothes and stood naked in front of me. She was uninhibited, and looked at me earnestly and with curiosity. She was amazed at how pale I was.

We'd left the light on, and it was still on when we fell asleep some time much later. I awoke as the sky began to brighten outside. The light was off now, and I saw the outline of Agnes's naked body against the milky light of the window. I got up and stood next to her. She had opened the little tilting window to the side, and pushed her hand through the narrow opening. We both stood there and watched her hand moving about outside, like a creature with a mind of its own.

"I couldn't get the window open."

"The apartment is temperature-controlled."

We were both silent. Agnes was tracing slow circling movements with her wrist.

"I could almost be your father," I said.

"Yes, but you're not."

Agnes pulled her hand back in and turned to me.

"Do you believe in life after death?"

"No," I said, "it would make everything some-how . . . meaningless. If life went on afterward."

"When I was little, my parents took me to church every week," said Agnes, "but I was never able to believe in it. Even though I sometimes wanted to. We had a Sunday school teacher, a small, ugly woman who had something wrong with her. I think she had a clubfoot. Once she told us about the time she'd lost her house key when she was a little girl. Her parents were at work, and she couldn't get into the house. So she'd said a prayer, and God had shown her where the key was. She'd lost it on her way home from school. After that, I sometimes prayed myself, but my prayers generally began, 'Almighty God, if you really exist . . .' More often, I would set myself little challenges. If I manage to stand on one leg for a quarter of an hour, or if I can take a hundred paces with my eyes shut, then whatever I want will happen. Even now, I sometimes go into a church and light a candle for the dead. Even though I don't believe in it. As a child, I always thought, why does that woman have a clubfoot if God loves her. It didn't seem fair."

"Maybe there is a sort of everlasting life," I said, and shut the window. The quiet sounds of the night abruptly ceased, and I felt we were in a small enclosed space again. "In a way, we do carry on living after we're dead. In the memories of other people, in our children, and in things we've created."

"Is that why you write books? Because you don't have any children?"

"I don't want to live forever. I really don't. I don't want to leave any traces when I die."

"You must," said Agnes.

"Come on," I said, "let's go back to bed. It's still early."

# 6

When I woke up again, it was almost noon. Agnes was asleep. She was lying on her back, and had the blanket pulled up over her face. When I got up, it woke her up, and when I stood in the shower, she came into the bathroom, leaned against the sink, and said: "I can't believe what we did last night, even if it's only what millions of people do all over the world every second."

Agnes locked the door when she had her shower. When she came out, completely dressed, I asked her if she was shy of me.

"No," she said, "I always lock the door, even when I'm all alone. There was never a key to the bathroom in my parents' house. Sometimes they would go to the toilet while I was having a shower."

I shaved, and Agnes went downstairs to the shop to buy orange juice and bread for toast.

"The man stared at me," she said when she came back. "He must have remembered seeing us together last night. When I gave him the money, he licked his lips at me and rolled his eyes."

I made coffee and eggs and toast. Over breakfast, Agnes asked about my books. I showed them to her. She flicked through them, and said it was a pity she couldn't read German.

"I'm sure you're dying to know all about cigars and bicycles," I said.

"I'd like to be able to read what you write. You have long sentences in German, don't you?"

I felt a bit ashamed of what I had to show for my life up to that point. I showed Agnes a slim volume of short stories that I'd published many years ago, and told her about a few literary projects that were biding their time in my desk drawer. Years ago, I'd started writing a novel, but never got beyond the first fifty pages. Agnes asked me to tell her what it was about, and while I struggled to sum up what little I could remember of it, it suddenly seemed absurd to have these kinds of delusions at my age.

"I've given it up," I said. "It's years since I last worked on it. Sooner or later, you have to realize . . ."

"You shouldn't have given it up, the beginning sounds really interesting."

"I was never in control of my material. It was always artificial. I got drunk on the sound of my own words. Or it was like singing, when you forget about the words, and only think about the melody. Like in those Italian operas that no one can actually follow."

We ate in silence.

"Why did you bring your books with you to Chicago, then?" Agnes asked. "Do you read them?"

"No, I never look at them. Very rarely."

"Can you remember what they say? Do you know a lot about cigars?"

"Not really. When I take them down and look at them, it's not to read up on things. The books remind me of the time they were written. They're a kind of randomized memory. In the same way, luxury trains will always remind me of you and Chicago."

"You make it sound as though we'd already split up."

"Oh, sorry, I didn't mean it that way."

"A copy of my dissertation is going to end up in the library," said Agnes. "I like to think that everyone who's ever going to do work on the symmetry of symmetrical crystal groups is going to run into my name."

We walked to the library together.

"Have you ever been to Stonehenge?" Agnes asked.

"I went once," I said. "It was ghastly. It's right on a main road, and the whole place is incredibly commercialized. You can't even see the stones for souvenir stalls."

"I've never been there, but I read a theory about it once. It was a woman's, I forget her name. She said that the stones had no astrological or mythological significance at all, they'd just been put there by prehistoric men to leave a trace of themselves, a kind of reminder. They were afraid that nature would overwhelm them, and they would disappear. They wanted to leave something of themselves, a sign that someone had once been there, that there had been people."

"A pretty elaborate sign, if you ask me."

"And the pyramids were the same, and maybe the Sears Tower as well . . . Have you ever been in the forests around here?"

"No. I've never left the city."

"They're absolutely endless. All the trees are the same height. If you leave the trail, you get lost immediately. You could disappear and never ever be found."

"Oh, someone would come by sooner or later," I said.

"I was in the Girl Scouts when I was little," Agnes said. "My father made me, even though I hated it. Being with all the other girls. Once we went to a camp in the Catskills. We slept in tents, and had to dig a hole in the ground for a toilet. We built a rope bridge, and one of the girls fell, the girl who lived next door to me at home. I always hated her. She did badly at school, but she was good with her hands, and often used to help my father in the garden. He treated her like his own daughter, and always said he wished he could have had a girl like her. At first we thought she was OK after the accident. Jennifer was her name. Then, one morning, two or three days later, she was lying dead in the tent. It was horrible. Everyone cried, and one of the teachers had to walk into the nearest town. Some men came with a stretcher and took her away. We all went back in the bus, and everybody else was crying the whole way. All except me. I wasn't pleased that Jennifer was dead, but I wasn't sorry either. I was relieved to go home. Afterward, they were furious with me, it was as though I was to blame. My father was the worst. I'd never seen him cry before. If it was me that had died, I don't think he would have cried that much, or maybe not at all."

7

I went to New York for five days, to get some books I hadn't been able to find in Chicago. Since getting together with Agnes, I was starting to work a little better. Just knowing that she existed and that I was going to see her seemed to spur me on. Even though my book was about luxury trains, I could only afford a second-class ticket for the night train. It was pretty full, and I was glad that the seat next to me was empty. But then, at the second stop, in South Bend, an enormous fat woman came and sat in it. She was wearing a thin knitted sweater with Santa Claus appliquéd on it, and she smelled of rancid old sweat. Her flesh ballooned over the armrest between us, and even though I pressed myself against the wall of the car, I couldn't avoid her contact. I got up and walked to the bar near the front of the train.

I drank a beer. It was slowly getting dark outside. The scenery had something approximate or unfinished about it. When we went through a forest, I thought of what Agnes had said about being able to disappear in one of these forests and never be seen again. From time to time we passed houses that didn't stand alone but that didn't constitute a village either. There too, I thought, you might disappear and never be seen again. A young man started talking to me. He said he was a masseur, and was going to see his parents in New York. He told me about his work, and then some stuff about magnetism or aural therapy or something like that. I stood next to him looking out of the window, trying not to listen. When he offered me a cut-price massage, I went back to my car. The fat woman had turned onto her hip, and was taking up even more space. She had gone to sleep, and was breathing noisily. I clambered over her and squeezed into my seat. In the bag at her feet I saw a book called *What Good Girls Don't Do*. I cautiously pulled it out and started looking at it. Halfway through it, I came upon sketches of penises and vaginas and two diagrams that claimed to show male and female orgasms. As I pushed the book back into the woman's bag, she woke up. She smiled at me and whispered: "I'm going to see my lover."

I nodded, and she went on: "It's our first meeting. He's Algerian. We got in touch through an organization."

"Is that right," I said.

"Do you like my sweater? Doesn't it make me look attractive?"

"It's different."

"I need to go to sleep, so I look fresh and rested for tomorrow."

She giggled, turned onto her side, and was soon asleep again. Eventually I too fell asleep. When I woke up, it was starting to get light. The train was going along next to a wide river. I went to the dining car and got some coffee. Before long the fat woman turned up.

"May I?" she said, and sat down opposite me. "Don't you agree that trains are more comfortable than planes?"

"Sure," I said, staring out of the window.

"In six hours we'll be there," she said. "I'm too excited to sleep any more." She pulled a photograph out of her handbag and showed it to me. "There he is. His name's Paco."

"You ought to be careful. It's not every man you can trust."

"We've been writing each other letters for months. He plays the guitar."

"Do you know anyone else in New York?"

"I know Paco, and he's enough for me," she said, saying the name with a strange and affected drawl. Then she pulled a dog-eared letter out of her handbag and gave that to me. "Here. Read it."

I read the first couple of sentences, and handed it back to her. Paco was writing about some photograph that his lover had sent him.

"Do you think he loves me?" she asked.

"I'm sure it'll be fine," I said.

She smiled gratefully and said: "I can't believe anyone who writes such beautiful letters can be a bad man."

# 8

I came back from New York on a Sunday morning. I had taken the night train again, and called Agnes from the station.

"Will you come over?" she said. "I've got something to show you."

It was the first time she'd asked me to her place. Even though she'd given me precise instructions, it took me a long time to find the street. Her cheeks were flushed with excitement when she opened the door. She beamed and asked me in.

"First we'll eat," she said. "Sit down, I'm almost ready."

While she was busy in the kitchen, I looked around her room. You could tell Agnes had gone to some trouble to make it all cozy. The mattress in an alcove had some cuddly toys on it, and there was a big desk in the window with the computer. The round dining table in the middle of the room was set, and there were flowers and candles on it. The fireplace had been filled in. On the mantelpiece were some family snapshots and a picture of Agnes in a gown, which was probably taken at her graduation. She was looking straight into the camera, but even though she was smiling, her face seemed vague and inscrutable.

"You used to have longer hair," I called through into the kitchen.

Agnes poked her head around the corner and said: "Are you talking about my graduation picture? My father took that. I was drunk."

"You don't look it."

"I haven't got a head for it. Can you wait another minute. Look around."

She vanished back into the kitchen. I walked over to the window, which was open a crack. It was noon, drizzling outside. The street was deserted. I turned around. There were potted plants all over, but the room still had an unlived-in feel, as though no one had set foot in it for years. Now I noticed that Agnes had hardly any books. Apart from a little row of textbooks and computer manuals that were lined up on a low shelf, I could only see the *Norton Anthology of Poetry*.

There were a couple of posters on the walls, an Alpine landscape by Kirchner, and a repulsive theater poster.

"*Mörder, Hoffnung der Frauen*," said Agnes, carrying a bowl out of the kitchen. She said it in German; it was strange to hear her speaking my language. It made her voice sound older and raspier. "That's a poster of Oskar Kokoschka's," she said, in English once more.

"Do you know what the title means?" I asked.

Agnes nodded. "I know what it means, but I'm not sure why he wanted to say such a thing."

"Me neither."

"That was when I met Herbert," said Agnes, pointing at the photograph, "at the graduation party. It was three years ago. He was working for a catering company."

"Is he a waiter?" I asked.

"Actor," said Agnes. "My parents had come up from Florida specially. They could have stayed with me, but my father insisted on getting a room in a hotel. He didn't want to be any trouble, my mother said. She always made excuses for him. When he noticed that Herbert was flirting with me, he was mad. He behaved like a moron, found fault with everything, and wanted me to leave with them. I was pretty tired and drunk by then, and I wouldn't have minded going home. But he'd annoyed me so much all evening that I stayed just to annoy him back, and Herbert came up and asked me in front of him whether I'd dance with him after supper. There was a band at the celebration, but I had to wait a long time for Herbert to finish work. My father made a scene, and called me a tart. Can you imagine? By the time they finally left, my mother was crying."

"Then what?" I said.

"I think I was a bit in love," said Agnes. "We danced together for quite a long time. Herbert was kissing me. Then he drove me home. But nothing happened. I think he would have been too much in awe of my gown."

"Too much, eh?" I said, and Agnes laughed and winked at me.

"It cost him his job, because he was so late back with the van and all the dirty plates and everything."

"Do you still see him?"

"He's found a job in New York. He's working as an announcer in a shopping center, and he's hoping to be discovered."

After lunch, Agnes made me sit next to her at her desk. She turned on the computer, and opened a text file.

"Read it," she said.

I started reading, but no sooner had I skipped over the first couple of sentences than she interrupted me and said: "You see, I've written a story too. I'd like to write more of it. What do you think?"

"Give me a chance," I said. But she was too nervous to sit next to me quietly.

"I'll go and make us some coffee."

I read.

*I have to go. I get up. I leave the house. I take the train. A man is staring at me. He sits down next to me. He gets up when I get up. He follows me when I get out. When I turn around, I can't see him, that's how close he is to me. But he doesn't touch me. He follows me. He doesn't speak. Day and night, he's always with me. He sleeps with me, without touching me. He is in me, filling me. When I look in the mirror, all I can see is him. I can't recognize my hands or my feet anymore. My clothes are too small, my shoes pinch me, my hair has gotten lighter, my voice darker. I have to go. I get up. I leave the house.*

I read the text quickly and carelessly. I was impatient. Agnes came back from the kitchen, smiling timidly. We moved back to the table. The candles had almost burnt down.

"Well?" she said.

"Coffee?" I said. I didn't feel like criticizing her text, and resented her for making me. When she apologized, and poured me a coffee, I felt embarrassed.

"Listen," I began. I couldn't endure her expectant gaze, and picked up my coffee and went over to the window. "Listen, you can't just sit down and expect to write a novel in a week. I don't design computer software either."

"It's only a short story," pleaded Agnes.

"I can't judge it," I said, "I don't want to. I'm not a writer."

Agnes didn't say anything, and I looked out of the window.

"It reminds me of a mathematical formula," I said. "It's like you've got an unknown X in your head that you're trying to find. The story keeps narrowing down, like a funnel. And sooner or later you'll get your result, and it'll be zero."

I went on like that for a while, and probably believed what I was saying. It was nothing really to do with the story anymore. Maybe it really wasn't any good, but it was certainly better than anything I'd written in the last ten years.

"You don't even read anything," I said finally, "you've got no books. How are you going to write if you don't read?"

Silently Agnes cut the apple pie she'd baked for me.

"Do you want some ice cream with it?" she asked, without looking up. We ate.

"Good pie," I said.

Agnes got up and went over to her computer. There were stars on the screen, little points of light that kept radiating out. When Agnes moved the mouse, her story reappeared. She touched a couple of keys, and the text went away.

"What are you doing?" I asked.

"I wiped it," she said. "Forget it. Shall we go for a walk?"

We walked around her neighborhood. The rain had stopped, but the streets were still all wet. Agnes showed me where she bought food, where she did her laundry, the restaurant she often went out to in the evenings. I tried to imagine what it was like, feeling at home in these particular streets, but I couldn't do it.

Agnes said she liked living here, she liked the neighborhood, even though it wasn't pretty and she didn't have any friends there. When we got back to her apartment, she pulled a stack of murky glass slides out of a drawer.

"This is my work," she said.

At a glance, all the glass slides seemed to be evenly murky, but when I looked at them more closely, I saw there were patterns of tiny dots in the murk. On each glass plate, there was a different pattern.

"Those are X-rays of crystal lattice structures," said Agnes. "The actual arrangements of atoms. Almost everything is symmetrical at some level."

I handed the plates back to her. She went over to the window and held them up against the light.

"The mystery is the void at the center," she said, "what you don't see, the axes of symmetry."

"But what's that got to do with us?" I asked her. "With you and me, with life. We're asymmetrical."

"There's always a reason for asymmetry," Agnes said. "It's asymmetry that makes life possible. The difference between the sexes. The fact that time goes in one direction. Asymmetries always have a reason and an effect."

I hadn't heard Agnes sounding so impassioned about anything before. I threw my arms around her. She held the slides up in the air, to keep them safe, and said: "Careful, they'll break."

In spite of her warning, I picked Agnes up in my arms and carried her over to the mattress. She got up quickly to put her slides away, and then she returned, got undressed, and lay down next to me. We made love, and then it was dark outside. I spent the night with her.

Early in the morning, I was woken up by a knocking in the pipes. I sat up and saw that Agnes was awake as well.

"Somebody's sending Morse code signals," I said.

"That's the steam central heating; my place isn't temperature-controlled like your place. The heat makes the pipes expand, and they make that noise."

"Doesn't it bother you? You can't sleep with that noise going on, can you?"

"No, I like it," said Agnes. "I feel I'm not alone when I wake up at night."

"But you're not alone."

"No," said Agnes. "Not now."

# 9

"I've been thinking," said Agnes, when we met up a few days later. It was the evening of the 3rd of July, and we had gone for a walk along the shore of Lake Michigan. The Independence Day celebrations begin the night before in Chicago, with music and fireworks. Grant Park was swarming with people, but here, only a bit further north, the lakeside walk was almost deserted. We sat down on the quayside and looked out at the lake.

"Why did you stop writing," asked Agnes, "stop writing for yourself, I mean?"

"I don't know. I didn't have anything to say. Or I wasn't good enough. I just stopped one day."

"Wouldn't you like to start again?"

"Like to? That doesn't really get you anywhere . . . Why do you ask? Do you want a famous boyfriend?"

"Boyfriend," said Agnes, "that sounds strange." She drew up her legs, and rested her chin on her knees.

"I had the feeling you were jealous when I showed you my story."

"I'm sorry. I really am. I got angry, I wasn't fair to you."

"That's all right. You showed me your book of short stories."

"That book sold all of one hundred and eighty-seven copies."

"That's not important. But you can write stories. Come on, let's go back."

It was beginning to get dark as we got up to go. The downtown skyscrapers, backlit by the low sun, blended into one, like a colossal fortress.

There was a group of Hispanics, maybe a family, that had lit a fire on the shore, and was celebrating. Agnes took my arm.

"Couldn't you write a story about me?" she asked.

I laughed, and she laughed with me.

"If it's immortality you want, you ought to find some-one more famous than me."

"Two hundred copies are enough. Even if it's never published. It would be like having my portrait painted. You saw the photographs of me. There's not a single decent picture of me. One that shows me as I am."

"Shall I write a poem to you?" I asked. *So long as men can breathe, or eyes can see, so long lives this, and this gives life to thee.*"

"Not a poem," said Agnes, "a story."

We were back at the Doral Plaza. The little shop was shut.

"Have you ever used the stairs?" Agnes asked.

"No," I said, "why should I?"

"How do you know you really live on the twenty-seventh floor?"

We walked up the stairs, counting the floors. The staircase was narrow and painted yellow. When we stopped for a rest on the twentieth floor, we heard some distant footsteps. We held our breath, but the steps suddenly stopped and a door slammed, and there was silence again.

"I don't like elevators," said Agnes, "I'd rather feel the ground under my feet."

"I think they're pretty practical," I said as I began climbing again, "just imagine . . ."

"I wouldn't want to live that high anyway," said Agnes, setting off after me; "it's not good."

We duly found my apartment on the twenty-seventh floor. I flopped exhausted onto the sofa. Agnes got herself a glass of water, and brought me a beer.

"I've never written any stories about living people," I said, "at the most I might have based characters on people I knew. But you need to have freedom in the actual story. Otherwise you'd be writing journalism."

Agnes sat down beside me.

"And the stories you wrote, they ended up not having to do with the people you thought of when you started?"

"No, they did," I said, "or with my impression of those people. Maybe too much. My then girlfriend left me because she recognized herself in one of the stories."

"Really?" asked Agnes.

"No," I said, "that was just the version we put out for public consumption."

Agnes pondered.

"Write a story about me," she said, "so I know what you think of me."

"I have no idea what might come out," I said, "I haven't any control over it. We might both be disappointed."

"I'll take my chances," said Agnes, "you just need to write it."

I was in love, and saw no reason not to sacrifice a couple of days and write a story. Agnes's enthusiasm had made me curious whether the experiment would succeed, whether I still had any ability to write a story.

"OK, let's start," said Agnes, "a love story with you and me."

"No," I said. "Remember, I'm doing this. And before I start, I want to go and see the fireworks."

Agnes said she didn't care about any fireworks, and could I not begin immediately. I took a piece of paper, and wrote.

*On the evening of July 3, we went up on the roof and watched the fireworks together.*

The elevator went up to the thirty-fourth floor, and from there a small staircase led up to the roof. There was a wooden deck underfoot, almost blackened by the sun and the rain. We went up to the guardrails and looked down. Far below us, we could see cars drive past, and tiny pedestrians negotiating the evening traffic. We could see the lake from here, and Grant Park, where dozens of little fires were burning.

"All those people," said Agnes. "They haven't a clue that we're observing them."

"It wouldn't make any difference if they did."

"They could hide," said Agnes. "Do you know what time the fireworks start?"

"No, I don't. When it's a bit darker. Are you cold?"

"No," she said, and lay down on a wooden bench. "Do you come up here a lot?"

I sat down next to her. "At first, I used to come up here almost every day. Now I don't go all that much. Not at all, I suppose."

"Why not?" asked Agnes. "You can see the stars from here."

The fireworks began. Agnes stood up, and we walked back over to the railing, even though the rockets were going off high over our heads, and we could just as well have watched them from the middle of the roof.

"How long has Switzerland been independent?"

"I don't know," I said, "it's hard to say."

# 10

When we were back inside the apartment, we felt cold.

"Now you have to begin the story," said Agnes.

"OK," I said, "then you'll have to sit for me."

We went into the study. Agnes sat in the basket chair by the window, and, as though she was having her picture taken, she swept the hair out of her face, straightened her blouse, and smiled at me. I sat down at the computer and looked at her. Once more, even though she was smiling, I was astonished by the seriousness in her face and her expression, which I didn't know how to read.

"How would you like to look?" I asked.

"I want it to be accurate," she said. "But nice as well. You are in love with me after all, aren't you?"

I wrote.

*The first time I saw Agnes was in April this year, in the Chicago Public Library.*

"What did you write?" she asked.

I read her the sentence, and she was satisfied.

"You don't need to sit for me anymore," I said, "I just wanted to look at you in peace for a while."

"I don't mind," said Agnes.

"But it stops me from writing, if you sit there and watch me. Will you make us a coffee?"

Agnes went into the kitchen. When she came back, I read her what I had written.

*The first time I saw Agnes was in April this year, in the Chicago Public Library. I noticed her right away, from the moment she came and sat down opposite me in the reading room. Her awkward movements didn't seem to fit with her slim, delicate body. Her face was fine-boned and pale, with dark hair that fell to her shoulders. We looked at each other for a moment, and I saw her startled blue eyes. When she left the reading room, I followed her. We met again on the library stairs, and I asked her if she'd like a cup of coffee.*

*Our conversation developed unusually quickly. We were talking about love and death, before we even knew each other's names. She had strong opinions. My cynicism provoked her, and in her agitation she grew flushed and appeared even more vulnerable.*

Agnes was annoyed. "You didn't have to put that."

"Do you want me to write or not? It was your idea."

"I always used to blush when I was a child. I got teased and laughed at for it in school. My father hated it when I was teased."

"Didn't you?"

"You get used to it. I read a lot. And I did well at school."

"Would you like me to take it out, then?"

"Yes, please. And do you have to write about my childhood? It's only a story after all. Can't I just turn up in the library one day, and just be me? The way I am?"

"Sure," I said, "you'll spring from my head fully formed, like Athene from Zeus, all wise and beautiful and unapproachable."

"I don't want to be unapproachable," said Agnes, and she kissed me on the mouth.

# *11*

Over the next few weeks, I neglected my luxury trains. I was writing Agnes's story, writing how everything happened, and when we met up, I would read her my new chapters.

It was amazing how many things there were that Agnes and I remembered differently, or had experienced differently. We were often unable to agree, and though I generally had my way, I sometimes wondered whether she wasn't right after all.

For instance, we couldn't agree for a long time on what restaurant we had gone to the first time. Agnes was sure it was the Indian, and I was sure it was the Chinese opposite. I even thought I could remember my order. Then Agnes remembered she'd noted our date in her pocket diary, and the entry proved that I was wrong.

Some of the things I went into great detail about were of no significance to her. Other things that mattered to her weren't even included by me, or only mentioned in passing, like the dead woman we saw in front of the restaurant that evening. I mentioned the incident, but nothing more. I didn't say we'd later learned her story, or that we'd even attended her funeral later. Agnes had been very moved by her, and wrote several letters to her relatives.

I didn't mention Herbert in my story either, and Agnes said I was jealous, and that seemed to make her happy. On the odd occasion when we did talk about him, she dodged my questions, or gave general answers. She didn't like talking about her childhood, but when she was in a good mood and told me about some incident from it, she would stop as suddenly as she'd begun. By the end of August, when I'd caught up with the present, my text was already far too long.

There had been a long period of wet weather when, in early September, a cool, dry wind blew south across the lake, and scattered the clouds. We had decided to spend the day outdoors. Agnes had gone home to change, and when she came back, she buzzed me from downstairs so as not to waste any more time. She was sitting in one of the black-leather armchairs in the lobby, and looked oddly unfamiliar. She was wearing dark blue knicker-bockers, a white T-shirt, and stout shoes that looked as though they'd never been worn.

"We're only going to a park," I said, "not the Rockies."

"It's not a park, it's a forest," said Agnes. "I thought we would go hiking."

"That's OK," I said, and when Agnes looked doubt-fully at my town shoes: "I can walk in these for hours."

There were lots of lakes and canals in the park, and we kept stopping and sitting down to talk by the side of them. I told Agnes she looked different somehow, and she said she'd trimmed her bangs. Then I had to hold on to her while she peered over the edge of the little lake and studied her reflection in the water.

"Is it so awful?" she asked.

"I don't think it was just that."

We had brought a blanket and sandwiches with us, and in the late afternoon, we lay down in a sunny clearing. We had something to eat, then Agnes fell asleep, but I didn't feel tired and sat up to smoke a cigarette. The low sun cut through the trees and cast little splashes of light on her as she slept. I looked at her, and didn't recognize her. Her face was like an unfamiliar landscape. The eyes were like a couple of mounds in the flat craters of their sockets; the nose was a delicate ridge that gradually climbed and widened to a peak, where it collapsed toward the mouth. I noticed for the first time the soft hollows on either side of her eyes, and the roundness of her cheeks and chin. Her whole face looked strange and unfamiliar, and yet I felt I was seeing it more truly and directly than I'd ever seen it before. Though I didn't touch Agnes, I had the frightening and yet still intoxicatingly beautiful feeling that I was all around her like a second skin, and could feel her whole body pressed directly against mine.

I stayed perfectly still. The last of the sun's rays had gone from the clearing, and it was getting chilly. Agnes's mouth twitched, and her brow creased for a brief moment. Then she awoke. I lay down next to her and held her tightly to me.

"What is it?" she asked, and looked into my eyes with astonishment.

I didn't look back at her, but I kept holding her, squeezing her even more tightly, kissing her face and throat. She smiled.

"I had a weird feeling of being terribly close to you just now," I said to her.

"And are you still?" she asked.

I didn't reply, and Agnes didn't say anything either, and just held me as though she was afraid I would withdraw from her again. Later on, I told her I loved her, but that didn't feel like enough, and because I didn't know how else I might express whatever I was feeling, I didn't say anything else, and neither of us said much that evening.

# *12*

My love for Agnes had changed, and was different now from anything I'd experienced before. I felt an almost physical dependency on her; when she wasn't there I had a dismaying sensation of not being complete. Whereas in my previous relationships I'd always insisted on having a lot of time for myself, it wasn't possible for me to see enough of Agnes. Ever since our hike in the park, I thought about her all the time, and only really calmed down when she was with me, and when I could look at her and touch her. Then, when she was with me, I felt intoxicated, and everything around me, like the air and the light, seemed painfully clear and close, and time itself got to seem concrete and actual as it passed. For the first time in my life, I had the sensation that something out-side me, something strange and incomprehensible, was entering me.

I began observing Agnes, and I saw how little I actu-ally knew her. I noticed the private rituals she celebrated, apparently unaware of them. When we went out to restaurants, and the waiter or waitress had set the table, Agnes always adjusted her cutlery. When her food was brought in, she lifted the plate on her two index fingers and balanced it in the air for a moment, as though looking for its center of gravity, and then put it down again.

She never touched strangers, and avoided being touched by them. However, she couldn't stop touching objects. She would brush against furniture and buildings with her hands when walking past them. Smaller things she would practically grope, as though she couldn't see them. Sometimes she would sniff them too, but when I drew her attention to that, she would claim not to realize.

When she was reading, she would be so immersed in her text that she wouldn't reply if I spoke to her. Echoes of what she was reading, intimations of feelings, would chase across her face. She would smile, she would press her lips together. On occasions, she would sigh, or frown with annoyance.

Agnes seemed to be aware that I was observing her, but she didn't say anything. I think she enjoyed it. Sometimes she would respond to my amazed expression with a smile, but never with vanity.

A few days after our excursion to the lake, the story moved into the future. Now Agnes was my creation. I felt the new freedom lend wings to my imagination. I planned her future for her, the way a father would plan his daughter's. She would write a dazzling doctoral thesis, and be a star in the university. We would be happy together. I could see that eventually Agnes would come to life in my story, and go her own ways, and that no plan of mine could prevent that. I knew such a moment would come, if the story was any good, and I was both pleased and apprehensive at the prospect.

We didn't see each other for a few days, but I'd thought about Agnes the whole time, and gone on with the story. When my publisher called me to ask how I was getting on with the book, I tried to set him at ease, and said I'd had difficulties getting hold of certain documents. He said he'd scheduled the book for next autumn, and I promised to deliver the manuscript by Christmas. I put the phone down, rang Agnes, and asked her over.

"You'll be wearing your navy-blue dress," I said.

"What do you mean?" she asked in amazement.

"I've overtaken the present," I said. "I know the future." She laughed.

# 13

When Agnes came over the next day, she was duly wearing her short navy dress. It was cold and rainy, but she
said: "Orders are orders," and when I apologized she
merely laughed.

"*We went into the living room, and Agnes threw her
arms around me, and kissed me for a long time, as though
afraid of losing me*," I quoted. And Agnes embraced me
just as I had described, only she was laughing as she did,
and wasn't afraid. I freed myself and went into the kitchen
to finish making supper.

"Can I help?" she asked.

"No," I said. "*Agnes sat in the living room, listening
to my CDs, while I cooked supper.*" I had bought a bottle
of champagne, though neither of us particularly liked it.

"What are we celebrating?" asked Agnes.

"*It was a very special day for us. I had decided* . . . But
first let's eat."

"That's mean," she said, "first you make me all curious, and then you say . . ."

"I'm sorry," I said, "we can talk about whatever it is
afterward."

We talked about other things, but I could see that Agnes was in suspense. She ate faster than she usually did, and when we were finished, we didn't clear the table and just left our dirty plates where they were. I moved over to the sofa, and took a piece of paper from my pocket.

"Come here," I said, but Agnes sat down on a chair by the window.

"First of all I want to know what I have to do," she said. "I don't want to make any mistakes."

I couldn't see her face from where I was sitting. Her voice sounded a little distant.

"Go on," she said, "read!"

"*We sat together on the sofa,*" I read, and stopped for a moment. But Agnes didn't move, and so I continued: "*Agnes was leaning back against me. I kissed her neck. I had thought about this moment for a long time, but when I opened my mouth to speak, I forgot the little speech I had prepared. So I just said: 'Will you come and live with me?'*" I stopped, waited, and looked at Agnes. She didn't say anything.

"Well?" I asked.

"What does she reply?" she asked.

I read on: "*Agnes sat up, and scrutinized me. 'Do you mean that?' she finally asked. 'Of course,' I replied.* I've been wanting to ask you for a long time, but I thought . . . you're so independent . . ."

Agnes got up and walked over to the sofa. She sat down beside me and said: "Are you sure it'll work out?"

"Yes, I am," I replied. "When we were by the lake, I felt we were so close, and since that time, I've often felt lonely when I'm here by myself. Couldn't you live with me? I mean . . . we'd have more space here than in your apartment."

"Yes," she said. "Yes. Is that all right? Are you happy?" She laughed and said: "Now let's see how the story unfolds." She took the piece of paper out of my hand, read it, and then she said indignantly: "*Grateful? Why should I be grateful to you?*"

She jabbed me in the ribs.

"I was only kidding," I said, "I've changed it since."

"Ah, this part's better," she said. *"We drank champagne. Then we made love, and at midnight we went out on the roof to look at the stars."*

It was raining that night, so we couldn't see any stars. Agnes caught a chill from going up on the roof in her short dress. But at the end of September, she moved in with me. The lease on her own apartment ran till next spring, and so she left most of her things there, and just brought a couple of suitcases full of her clothes, her cello, and a few personal items with her.

# 14

Every morning, Agnes took the El to the university. I only got up once she was gone, went to my regular café to read the paper, and was back in the apartment shortly before noon. Agnes had lunch at the university. In the afternoons I wrote, or did research in the library.

It was a peaceful life, our days were all much the same, and we were happy. We had quickly gotten used to each other. I did the bulk of the housework, cooked the meals, and did Agnes's laundry. Writing took a back seat for a while. I was still collecting material for my train book, without much enthusiasm. When my editor called me again, I asked him to put off the delivery date. First of all he complained and said I was wrecking his entire autumn schedule. But I said I hadn't had a proper vacation for years, and I needed a break so that the book would be really good. Finally he consented, and then he even said it was probably for the best, as books about trains sold better in the spring than they did in the autumn anyway.

I was also barely working on Agnes's story anymore. Sometimes we played the game we'd played that evening. Then I would type up a few sentences on the computer, and tell Agnes what she had to do and play my own part. We wore whatever clothes the story said we wore, and, like my characters, we would go out to the zoo or to a museum. But neither of us was much good as an actor and our rather uneventful life didn't lend itself really to being written about.

"Something needs to happen, to make the story a bit more interesting," I told Agnes one day.

"Aren't you happy as we are?"

"Sure I am," I said, "but happiness doesn't make for interesting stories. Someone once said that happiness writes white. It's fleeting and transparent, like smoke or fog. Do you know any painter who could paint smoke?"

We went to the Art Institute of Chicago, to see if we could find a painting of smoke or fog, or a painting of happy people. We stood for a long time in front of Seurat's *Un Dimanche d'été à l'île de la Grande Jatte.* Seurat hadn't painted happy people, but his picture radiated a kind of tranquillity that was the nearest approximation to what we were looking for. It's a picture of a riverbank on a Sunday afternoon. Some people are promenading, and others just sitting and relaxing on a meadow, among shady trees.

As we approached the picture, it crumbled before our eyes into a sea of tiny dots. The edges of the shapes melted away, and they flowed into one another. The colors in the painting weren't mixed, but assembled as they might have been on a tapestry. There was no black and no white. Every area contained all the colors, and it was only from a distance that it had any definition. "That's you,"

I said, pointing to a girl in the center of the painting, who was sitting on the grass, holding a bunch of flowers in her hands. She was sitting very upright, but she had lowered her head to look more closely at the flowers. She had a hat and parasol beside her, which she didn't need, as she was sitting in the shade.

"No, that's not me," said Agnes, "I'm the girl in the white dress. And you're the monkey."

"No, I'm the man with the trumpet," I said, "but no one can hear me."

"Everyone can hear you," said Agnes. "You can't shut your ears."

We went to a place that claimed to serve the best cheesecake in the whole of Chicago, but Agnes wasn't convinced, and said she would make a better one, with raisins in it.

"You paint happiness with dots," she said, "and unhappiness with stripes. If you want to describe our happiness, you'll have to do it with lots and lots of little dots, like Seurat. And you'll only be able to tell it's happiness if you step away from it."

# 15

The second Monday in October was Columbus Day, and we took advantage of the holiday to leave the city. I had suggested driving to New York, but Agnes said she wanted to go hiking, but a proper hike this time. That was fine by me, and as the forecast was also fine, we decided to take my little tent and go camping. On the map, we found a national park not very far from Chicago. We rented a car, and early on Friday morning, we drove south out of the city.

Agnes had borrowed a video camera from her professor, and while I was driving, she was pointing it out of the window, and filming God knows what. Outside Indianapolis, the traffic got heavier. Agnes was driving now, and I wanted to film her at the wheel.

"Don't," she said, "you'll only break it. My professor would murder me. It's his favorite toy."

"I won't break it," I said, "and how else am I going to get a shot of you."

"You write, and I'll film," said Agnes.

We were too early for the Indian summer, said the ranger at the entrance to the national park, and he suggested we have our hike in an area that had reverted to wilderness in the course of the last fifty years. At the beginning of the century, he said, people had still been farming there, but in the thirties, during the Depression, they had all upped sticks and emigrated, and the state had bought up the area, and turned it into a wilderness.

"How do you do that?" asked Agnes.

"Just by letting it go," said the ranger. "Within a few years, Nature reclaimed everything. Civilization is only a thin veneer, and unless you look after it and keep it up, it cracks."

Agnes filmed the ranger's little cabin, and the ranger showing me where to go on the map. He waved the camera away and laughed, and Agnes laughed as well. Then he said we should take care, and handed us a leaflet about poisonous plants and wild animals. People tended to underestimate the dangers, he said, and Nature didn't fool around.

"Why did you film the park ranger and not me," I asked, as we drove into the park along a narrow forest road.

"He's a witness," said Agnes.

After a few miles, we reached a parking lot, where we stopped. It was almost noon when we started on our hike. We walked for hours through wooded terrain. Sometimes we thought we were on paths, but they gave up on us all of a sudden, and we were back to following compass directions through the forest.

"We ought to break off twigs," said Agnes, "so we find our way back."

"We're not going back," I said, "not the same way."

From time to time, we passed ruined farmsteads, places where the trees seemed younger and not so close together. It was beginning to get dark as we came over the crest of a hill, and saw the lake in front of us where we planned to make camp. It took us almost another hour before we finally reached its shores.

The sun had gone down, and it was getting chilly. The soil by the edge of the lake was sandy, and that's where we pitched our tent. Then we gathered firewood that was lying all around. Within a few minutes, we'd collected a great pile of it.

"I'll light the fire," said Agnes. "My father taught me how."

She made a little pyramid out of branches, pushed a handful of kindling into it, and said: "One match."

And she did it, she lit the fire with just one match. I heated soup on my little gas stove. We sat down on one of the mats, and ate and looked out over the lake, which was calm and dark. Occasionally, we heard a fish jumping, and once a plane flew by, far away.

Even though we were sitting right by the fire, Agnes was shivering. She was getting her sleeping bag, she said, and walked over to the tent. As soon as she had left the circle of firelight, she was gone from sight. I heard a sudden groan and a noise. I leapt up and found Agnes lying on the ground, only a few yards away. Now, facing away from the light, I could see her clearly enough. She was lying on the wet sand, with her legs strangely twisted. I lifted her up, almost falling over myself in the process, and carried her back to the mat. Even in the warm light of the fire, her face and her lips were chalk-white. I stuck my hand up her heavy woollen sweater and felt her heart going feebly. Her brow was clammy and cold. I sat down next to her, and kept calling her name, and stroking her head.

I was terrified. We had to be many hours from the nearest habitation, and I couldn't possibly find my way to it through the forest, in the middle of the night. I got the water bottle, and dribbled a bit of water into Agnes's half-open mouth. Then I thought it was idiotic giving water to someone who was unconscious, and I pulled her head up to me, and started to shake her. She felt heavy and floppy in my arms. Finally, I felt her beginning to resist the shaking, and slowly she came around.

"Was I unconscious?" she asked.

"I thought you . . . I thought something had happened to you," I said.

"My circulation," she said, "maybe I didn't have enough to eat. It's nothing to worry about."

I wanted to carry her back to the tent, but she refused, saying she wasn't sick. She didn't say much more than that on that evening, only that she was tired, and that she was feeling better.

# 16

When I woke up the next morning, Agnes was already awake. She said she felt sick, and could I get her some water. After she'd drunk it, she felt better and seemed completely restored. She yawned and stretched in her sleeping bag, while I knelt over her and watched. Only then did I notice that her face was scratched from her fall of the night before.

"You look like a savage," I said, and she threw both her arms around my neck, and pulled me down to her.

"Come in my sleeping bag and make me better," she said.

It was cold in the tent, and our breath made clouds, but we didn't feel cold. We had unzipped both sleeping bags, and laid one of them on the ground, the other over us like a blanket.

"Are you sure there's no one around?" asked Agnes.

Then the sun hit the tent, making it very bright and quickly warming it up. By the time we finally crept outside, it was so warm that Agnes got undressed and washed in the cold water of the lake. Then we made love again, out on the sandy shore, and Agnes washed again, and so did I, because I was all covered with sand.

"Don't you feel much more naked, out in the open," I said.

"But you could live like that," said Agnes, "naked and close to the earth."

"Wouldn't you be scared of disappearing in Nature? Getting dragged under?"

"No," she said, splashing me, "not today."

We left the lake, and walked on through the forest. In a long narrow valley, we came upon some rusted old railroad tracks. It was good walking on the former embankment. The valley widened out, and on either side of the tracks we saw the decrepit ruins of some wooden houses. We walked around, looking at them.

"How long do you think it will be until there are no more traces of human habitation?" asked Agnes.

"I don't know. Everything gets overgrown, but there's stuff left underneath if you look. Broken glass, wire, things like that."

The doors were boarded up, and there were signs warning you not to go inside. When we went into a little outbuilding, a wall of which had collapsed, a large bird flapped out into the open, with angry squawks. It gave us a shock. The rotten boards of the collapsed wall were lying on the ground. In one corner of the outbuilding, where it backed onto the main dwelling, was a heap of dry leaves. Beside it was a ring of soot-covered stones, a little hearth. The ground was strewn with rusty old tin cans and a few broken bottles.

"Do you think someone's living here still?" Agnes asked.

"The tin cans look pretty old to me. Not fifty years old, though. Maybe some other hikers came and stayed here."

"Perhaps there are people still living in this area that no one knows about. It must be hard to check up on that."

"Oh, there'd be smoke from the chimneys. You'd see that from an airplane."

"I wouldn't want to spend the night here," said Agnes. "I couldn't help feeling I was staying in someone else's house. Our generation will leave only its rubbish behind."

On the edge of the abandoned settlement we found a ruined church. Behind it was a small graveyard. The trees in it were almost as dense as in the forest, which stretched up the hill, immediately beyond. Most of the gravestones had been uprooted, and were lying on the forest floor. We made out a few names and dates.

"The dead don't know their village was abandoned," said Agnes.

"Don't you want to film any of it?" I asked.

"No," she said, "you can't go filming in a graveyard." She leaned against a tree trunk.

"Just imagine, in a few weeks all this will be covered in snow, and then no one will come for months, and it'll be completely peaceful and abandoned. Do you know that freezing's supposed to be a good way to die?"

We walked on, all that day and part of the next. The sky was clouded over, and we were relieved to hit the parking lot early in the afternoon of the third day. Agnes slept on the drive home. Shortly after Indianapolis, it started to rain, and it was still raining when we reached Chicago.

# 17

It rained for several days, and we'd begun to think winter had arrived, when it got warmer again. It smelled like summer, and the city lay in golden light. Agnes was away at the university, and I walked to Grant Park. I'd brought some sandwiches with me, and ate them sitting on a bench. I wandered over to the planetarium, and then back. I was wearing a warm jacket, and when I got back to the apartment, I was sweaty and tired. I made myself a coffee, but it didn't wake me up, just made my heart go. I sat down at the computer anyway. The low sun dazzled me. I shut the blinds. The air conditioner was humming. I wrote.

*One Sunday in November, we went to Lincoln Park Zoo, on the lake. It was one of those warm days that Chicago sometimes gets, even late in the year. We looked at the animals for a while.*

*"I don't really like zoos," said Agnes, "they make me sad. I haven't been in one for so long that I'd forgotten how sad they are."*

*We went on strolling around, no longer looking at the animals much. When it got to be lunchtime, we sat on a bench. We'd brought some sandwiches, and a thermos of tea, but we'd forgotten to bring any cups. When Agnes drank out of the flask, she spilled some tea on her sweater. She laughed, and I dabbed it off with my handkerchief. We looked at each other, and embraced each other, not saying anything.*

*"Will you marry me?" I asked.*

*"Yes," she said straight out, and neither of us seemed surprised by my sudden question.*

I didn't know how to go on from that point. As I was still feeling tired, I lay down on the sofa and tried to plan it in my head. I thought of how I would show Agnes my country, and how we would go hiking in the mountains there. I tried to picture our apartment, the furniture and the pictures we would choose together, and what it would be like when Agnes spoke her first few sentences of German.

I wasn't daydreaming. I was fully in control, and everything I thought to myself instantly became real. It was a feeling like walking along a narrow gorge that I couldn't leave. And if I tried to, I felt a kind of resistance, the presence of another will, some sort of elastic fetters that kept me from setting off in the wrong direction.

I saw Agnes standing in a narrow stairwell, without knowing where we were, or how she'd gotten there. The bare concrete walls were painted yellow, and the only light was from neon tubes on the landings. Agnes was huddled in a corner, and was looking at me fearfully and angrily at the same time.

Then she said: "I never wanted to marry you. You frighten me."

I slowly advanced toward her. "You never loved me," I said, "all the time we were together, you were thinking of that Herbert of yours."

Agnes pressed herself against the wall and, without taking her eyes off me, moved toward the staircase.

"You're insane!" she shouted. "You're sick!"

I wanted to move faster, but something was slowing me down. Agnes reached the stairs, turned away, and started running up them. I promptly lost her from sight, and could only hear her footfall and my own breathing, which was unusually loud. It was as though I was breathing in and out at the same time. I ran up the stairs, which seemed to have no end. Then I heard a door slam, and the next moment I had reached it. There was no door handle. I pressed my ear to the cold metal, and heard Agnes, very near me, whisper: "You're dead."

I hadn't shut my eyes the whole time; the room around me had become a blur. Something jerked me back to reality, and I stood up and went back to the study to write down what I'd seen. Now I could tell with each sentence whether Agnes was in agreement with it or not. Even though I knew I was being led by a dream character, her words still had a depressing effect on me. I'd never thought about asking Agnes to marry me in real life, but I still had the sense of somehow having guessed at her true feelings.

# 18

Every year, the university stages a big parade on Halloween, which is the last night of October. Agnes had often told me about it, the costumes she'd worn in previous years, and the wild party that took place afterward in the big hall of the university. Weeks before, she and the other members of her quartet had begun sewing their costumes. They were going to go as elves. I've always had an aversion to everything to do with masks and dressing up, and so I was relieved when I got an invitation to go to another Halloween party, given by Amtrak, the American railroad company, which would get me out of taking part in the parade. Agnes was disappointed.

"I'm relying on the cooperation of Amtrak for my work," I explained, "and if they invite me to something, I can't really refuse."

"But I invited you months ago," said Agnes.

"We can be together all the rest of the time," I said. "I'll only stay as long as I have to. I can go on to the party at the university afterward."

"You'll never find me there. And if you think I'm going to show you my costume ahead of time, you've got another think coming."

Agnes was still angry with me when she left the apartment on the evening of Halloween. She'd stuffed her costume into a gym bag. I told her to put some warm things on underneath, it was going to be cold that night. But she didn't reply, not even when I said I was sure I could get to the party at the university before midnight.

Amtrak's Halloween party was nothing special. But when I heard the parade going by outside, I felt I was well out of it. I went out onto the balcony, and tried to guess what costume Agnes was in. There were innumerable witches and skeletons and monsters and scarecrows. A few had luminous paint on them, and one or two were even on stilts.

"Is that really their notion of evil," said a woman who was standing next to me on the balcony. She had a faint French accent, and she added, sarcastically: "Those spirits don't come from the underworld, but out of the children's channel."

"You aren't from here, are you?"

"Certainly not," she said, laughing, "look at the way they're carrying on."

On the street below, a group of skeletons had begun a wild polonaise, and was rushing in and out of the spectators, who screamed as they tried to get out of the way. Then I saw a group of women wearing costumes made of white gauze and golden ribbons. They had small golden half masks over their upper faces. Even though I couldn't say for sure in all that confusion, I imagined that one of them moved a little like Agnes, with the same stiff gait.

"Even as a child, I didn't like masks," I said, taking a step backward.

"Look at those beauties down there," said the woman, "woolly tights and white gauze, every bridegroom's dream."

"I think they're elves," I said.

"Well, by their woolly long johns ye shall know them," said the woman. "My heart bleeds for American men."

"They don't all wear woollen underwear, you know," I said.

"Ooh, did I say something wrong? Is there a little girlfriend here, then? Come on, let's go inside, it's too cold here."

The woman went back into the room. I watched the elves for a moment, quite convinced that Agnes was among them. Then I went in after the woman, who was waiting for me beside the door.

"Little babies," she said. "May I introduce myself? I'm Louise. I work for Pullman Leasing."

Louise explained she was the daughter of a French grain merchant and an American woman. She had been living in Chicago for the past fifteen years, had studied here, and was now working in the public-relations department of Pullman Leasing, a company that rented out freight cars. She still hadn't gotten used to the mentality of people here, she said, even though she had spent half her life among them.

"They are savages," she kept saying, "decadent savages."

We talked about Europe and America, Paris and Switzerland. Then I told Louise about my book, and she suggested I should look in on her at work sometime. The Pullman that manufactured passenger cars had been the parent company of Pullman Leasing, and there were bound to be some documents in the company archives that I wouldn't come across in the public domain. I thanked her for her offer, and promised to take her up on it. When I left the party a little after midnight, she gave me her card, and wrote down her private telephone number on it. Then she kissed me on both cheeks, and said: "Call me. I haven't enjoyed a conversation so much for a long time."

# 19

After the Amtrak party, I went on to the university. The hall was full to bursting, and after I'd spent half an hour or so vainly looking for Agnes, I gave up and went home.

When Agnes got in sometime in the small hours, I woke up. I was relieved to see she wasn't dressed the same as those elves I'd seen from the balcony. She had trouble getting out of her costume, but when I tried to help her, she took a step back from me, and tore at it so violently that one of the seams split. The dress slid to the floor, and Agnes stood in front of me, swaying gently in pale beige thermal underwear. Her skin was shiny, in spite of the makeup she had put on for the occasion.

"Don't look at me like that," she said, "I'm drunk."

She went to bed, and pulled the sheets over her face. I lay down next to her, and tried to draw her toward me, but she turned away and mumbled: "Leave me alone. I'm dead tired."

In the morning, Agnes was in a bad mood. She had a headache and complained that she felt dizzy. The parade was over by ten o'clock, and she'd spent hours waiting for me. Finally she'd spotted me standing by the entrance, and shouted, but I failed to hear. By the time she'd fought her way across the room, I was gone. After that, she'd gotten drunk with her fellow elves from the Mathematical Institute.

"I saw the parade, and I thought I saw you too. But it wasn't you. It was an amazing parade."

"You can't say that unless you've taken part in it yourself."

Agnes spent almost the whole day in bed, reading, while I tried to get on with my work. When it was starting to get dark, she walked into my study. She went over to the window, and stood there, with her back to me.

"You feeling better?" I asked.

"Yes," she said, "I wanted to ask you something."

I switched off the computer, and swiveled around on my chair to face her. She continued to look out of the window. Finally she asked: "What will you do when you've finished your book?"

"Write the next one, I suppose."

"Where?"

"I don't know."

"What will happen with us, when you're finished."

I hesitated. Finally I said: "I guess we should talk about it."

"Yes," said Agnes, "that's what I'm trying to do."

Neither of us said anything. The temperature-control system seemed to be unusually noisy. Agnes hummed along to it, holding the note, and only stopping to breathe.

"What do you think?" I asked.

"What I think ... Doesn't that thing ever stop?"

"In summer it cools, and in winter it heats."

Neither of us said anything.

Then Agnes said: "I'm expecting a baby ... I'm pregnant. Are you pleased?"

I got up and went to the kitchen to get a beer. When I returned, Agnes was sitting at my desk, fiddling with a pen. I sat down next to her, without touching her. She took the bottle from me, and drank from it.

"Pregnant women aren't supposed to drink," I said, and laughed idiotically.

She gave me a punch on the shoulder. "Well?" she asked. "What do you say?"

"Well, it's not exactly what I had in mind. How come? Did you forget your Pill?"

"The doctor says it can happen, even if you're on the Pill. One percent or so of women on the Pill ..."

I shook my head and didn't say anything. Agnes started weeping softly.

"Agnes doesn't get pregnant," I said. "That's not what I ... You don't love me. Not really."

"How can you say that? It's not true. I've never ... never said that to you."

"I know you. Maybe I know you better than you know yourself."

"That's not true."

Perhaps to convince myself, I merely said: "She doesn't get pregnant."

Agnes ran into the bedroom. I heard her throwing herself on the bed, and sobbing loudly. I went in after her, and stood in the doorway. She said something I couldn't quite hear.

"What was that?"

"It's your baby."

"I don't want a baby. What would I want a baby for?"

"What shall I do? What do you want me to do? I can't change the fact."

I sat down on the bed, and put my hand on her shoulder.

"I don't need a baby."

"I don't need a baby either. But I'm getting one."

"Unless you do something about it," I said softly.

Agnes leapt up, and looked at me with a mixture of disgust and loathing.

"Do you want me to have an abortion?"

"I love you. We need to talk."

"You keep saying we need to talk. But you never talk."

"I'm talking now."

"Go, go away. Leave me alone. You and your story disgust me."

I left the room. I put on some warm clothes, and went out.

# 20

I walked for a long time beside the lake. At the end of Grant Park I found a café. There didn't seem to be anyone there, but when I went in, a waitress came out of the back room. She switched a light on, and asked me what I wanted. She brought me a coffee, and then disappeared again through the door behind the bar.

Outside, it was getting dark. The scenery on the other side of the big plate-glass windows was slowly obliterated, and before long all I could see was my own reflection in the glass.

Once before, many years ago, I thought I was going to be a father. A condom had split. I hadn't mentioned it to my girlfriend of the time, but I spent those weeks thinking about my impending fatherhood. The relationship in question had gotten to be rather shaky, but in that time of uncertainty I felt a new love for the woman, a tenderness and affection without any of the egoism I am always being accused of. When it finally turned out that my girlfriend wasn't pregnant, I was disappointed and blamed her for it, as though it were any fault of hers. Soon afterward, we broke up. I made unpleasant accusations against her that she didn't understand, couldn't possibly understand, because they were directed against another woman who only existed in my imagination. After that, I never wanted a baby.

I felt like writing, but in the rush I'd forgotten to take my notebook with me. I stood up to call the waitress and ask her for some paper. By the time she finally came, I just paid and left.

I went on, dropped into a bar, and then another. It was past midnight by the time I was back at the Doral Plaza. The doorman had been relieved, and a night doorman I'd never seen before stopped me and asked me what I wanted.

"I live here."

"What number?"

"It's on the twenty-seventh floor . . ."

I'd forgotten the number of my apartment and had to spell my name for the doorman. He carefully went through the list of residents until he found me. Then he apologized profusely and explained he was new, he was only doing his job, some of the tenants had complained that they had seen strangers in the building, and so forth.

"Out for a walk?" he said mechanically. "Must have been cold."

Agnes wasn't in the apartment. Some of her clothes weren't in the wardrobe, and her cello and toiletries were gone.

I lay down on the bed in my clothes. When I woke up, it was light. The telephone was ringing. It was Agnes. She said she was at home, in her apartment.

"What's the time? I've been asleep."

"I want to go over and get my things tonight, after class. Will you arrange to be out please. I'll leave the key with the doorman."

"What about the baby?"

"You don't have to concern yourself with that. It's my baby. When the time comes, I'll go to New York to be with Herbert."

It was afternoon already. Agnes seemed to have sorted everything out while I was sleeping. I had intended to apologize to her, but it was too late for that now. She had made up her mind.

"You don't want the baby," she said, "well, you're not having the baby."

And she hung up.

That evening, I went to the library. I took out some books, and sat down in the reading room to read. I couldn't concentrate at all, and noticed I was staring at the same page for minutes on end. I thought of Agnes, who was even then in my apartment, collecting her things together. So she'd called Herbert. I had always suspected that he'd meant more to her than she'd admitted. And he was clearly in love with her, I realized that from when she'd told me about the graduation party.

I stayed in the library until closing time. The apartment looked like it had before. Agnes had picked out her belongings from a heap of unironed clothing. She'd folded up my shirts and T-shirts and put them away in the closet.

# 21

After a few days, I called Agnes at her department. The secretary said she'd already gone home. I tried Agnes's apartment. A synthesized voice answered: *"We're sorry, this number is no longer available."* I waited, but the voice just kept on saying the sentence again. I wrote a letter to Agnes, and sent it to the university. I didn't get an answer.

One evening, a week or so after Agnes moved out, I waited for her in the street where she lived. I went into a coffee shop. From the place where I was sitting, I had a view of her front door. Agnes came back from class at her usual time. She was carrying a paper bag of grocer-ies, and disappeared into the house without looking back. A few seconds later, the light in her apartment went on. That was all. I waited a little longer, looking up at the lighted windows, until the waiter came over and asked if I wanted to order anything else.

"No," I said, and I paid and left.

November was rainy and cold. I went back to the café on Agnes's street again and again, until finally I was going there every day. I did my shopping in the shops in her neighborhood; on Saturdays I took my laundry to the Laundromat where Agnes did her washing. And I went back to the Indian restaurant where we had gone on our first date. I wasn't hoping to run into Agnes in any of these places, but I did feel closer to her there.

I went out almost every night, generally to a movie and a bar afterward. I rarely went to bed sober. I couldn't stand being in the apartment in the daytime. I spent entire days in the library, not working; I would order a thriller and take that into the reading room with me.

"Is that your work?" I heard a voice behind me ask. I turned around, and it was Louise. She took the book from my hands and said, with mock surprise: "*Murder with Mirrors* by Agatha Christie. Now if you were reading *Murder on the Orient Express*, that's at least got luxury trains in it."

Someone hissed at us to keep quiet.

"Shall we go for a coffee?" Louise asked, just as loud.

I followed her out of the reading room, and out of the building.

"Not here," I said, when I saw her heading for the coffee shop where I'd first had coffee with Agnes. But there wasn't another one, and I said it didn't matter, I was just being sentimental. I told Louise about Agnes, and that she'd left me. I didn't mention anything about the baby.

"I'm in no state to work," I said.

"Agnes," she said. "Funny name. Was she your little American girlfriend then, with the thermal underwear?"

"Yes, that's her."

"I think I ought to look after you a bit."

That same evening, Louise called me. Her parents were giving a party on Thanksgiving. It was going to be all business associates of her father's, and she would be only too pleased to have someone at the table who could talk about something other than the maize harvest and pork bellies. Louise lived with her parents in Oak Park, a wealthy suburb of Chicago. I said I'd be there.

After talking to Louise, I felt guilty somehow. It was as though I'd cheated on Agnes. Maybe that was why, for the first time in weeks, I pulled up the story about her on the computer, and read through everything I'd written so far. I'd never gotten past that scene on the stairs, the dream where Agnes told me she was scared of me. I wiped that last section, and read the zoo scene again, where we said we'd get married. And then I wrote.

*We kissed.*

*Then Agnes said: "I'm having a baby."*

*"A baby?" I said. "That's not possible."*

*"Yes, it is," she said.*

*"How come? Did you forget your Pill?"*

*"The doctor says it can happen even if you're on the Pill. One percent of women who are on the Pill..."*

*"It's not about you, or the baby," I said. "Please don't think... but I'm frightened of becoming a father. What do I have to offer a kid... I don't mean money." Neither of us said anything.*

*Finally Agnes said: "These things happen. You won't be any worse at it than anyone else. Won't we at least give it a go?"*

*"OK," I said, "we'll make it somehow."*

# 22

"Frank Lloyd Wright built around thirty houses in Oak Park," said Louise's father. He had a more marked French accent than his daughter.

"And Hemingway was born here," said Louise's mother. "Switzerland is a great little country. Last year we went to Stanton."

"St. Anton is in Austria, *chérie*," said her husband, turning to me again. "I hear you're a writer?"

"Louise has told us all about you," said the mother, "she likes you. And we're only too pleased if she settles down a bit. American men are so superficial. After all, I married a European myself."

She winked at her husband, who smiled modestly and said: "We met in Paris. My wife had gone to Europe to catch herself an aristocrat. She had to make do with me."

"I do hope you like turkey," said the mother, "we're having a traditional Thanksgiving dinner."

I was relieved when Louise came, slipped her arm in mine, and dragged me away from her parents.

"I'm just going to show him the garden," she said.

Her mother twinkled at me, and said: "I quite under-stand. You young people want to be alone together."

We strolled around the garden. There was an aqua-marine swimming pool under an enormous maple. The water was littered with its dead leaves. It was cold, and we shivered, but the sun still felt hot on my skin. The air was dry and crisp. When you looked up at the treetop, the sky between its bloodred leaves was almost black.

"I'm amazed by how much more colorful everything is here," I said, "the leaves, the sky, even the grass. Every-thing has more vitality than its counterpart in Europe. As though everything was still young."

"A man lives and dies in what he sees, says Paul Valéry, but he can only see what he thinks," Louise observed ironically.

"I really do think the colors here are different. Maybe it's to do with the air."

"My little pocket Thoreau. Try not to be so naïve. This country is no older or younger than any other."

"But I get the sense that more things are possible here."

"That's because you have no history in this place. The idea Europeans have of America is less to do with the place than with themselves. And of course vice versa. My mother's grandfather was the editor of the *Chicago Tribune*. From an old English family that could trace their descent back to the fourteenth century. So in a way, there's more history on my mother's side of the family than my father's. He came from a simple background. Made a good marriage. And there's my mother, rather pleased with herself for her European husband, even though he's exactly the sort of self-made man the Europeans suspect all Americans of being." She laughed.

"What did you tell your parents?" I asked. "They treated me like a prospective son-in-law."

"Oh, that's nothing. They'd love to have me married off. And they're pleased if I have a boyfriend who has some sort of sensible job. I told them you're a journalist, and you write books."

"Your mother said Hemingway was born around here."

"Yes, I know. She's a great name-dropper."

"Do you like Hemingway?"

"I'm not sure," said Louise. "I liked *A Farewell to Arms*, but that may have been because of the music and Gary Cooper."

After lunch, she showed me the apartment her parents had set up for her at the top of the house. Then she took me for a drive around the area, and showed me where Frank Lloyd Wright had worked, and where Hemingway was born. In the bookshop of the Hemingway house I found a copy of *A Farewell to Arms*, and gave it to Louise.

"You ought to read it," I said, "it's better than the film."

"And you ought to come and see me at work, so I can take you around our archives."

# 23

During my preliminary research in Switzerland, I'd kept coming across the name George Mortimer Pullman, but it wasn't until I got to Chicago that I discovered that the legendary constructor of sleeping cars was not only the inventor of the luxury train, but also made history with the model settlement that bore his name, south of Chicago. The small town of Pullman, which, from the provision of gas and water, through to its churches, was entirely the creation of the great industrialist, and which he ruled more as a father figure than as a proprietor, came to be the site for a series of strikes, civil disturbances, and violent protests that loomed large in the history of the labor movement in nineteenth-century America. In the end, they called in the army, but by then it was too late. Pullman's dream was in ruins.

The failure of Pullman's vision and the uprising of his labor force against the complete control of their lives by their employer fascinated me more than the company's celebrated railroad cars. It seemed that Pullman had planned for every contingency, except his workers' desire for freedom. He thought he had constructed a kind of paradisal community for them. But his Paradise didn't have a door, and as times grew harder and jobs were in ever shorter supply the workers felt they were little more than prisoners. Pullman never realized his mistake, and until the end of his life, he felt he was up against human ingratitude.

I didn't expect very much from the archives at Pullman Leasing, but I wanted to see Louise again, so I looked her up in her office a few days later. She gave me a tour of the gigantic site of the former factory, and showed me where, up until just after the Second World War, the railroad cars had been built. The factory halls had never been taken down; their demolition would have cost the company more than it could have earned from the sale of the site. Names were inscribed on the walls. On one pillar, some-one had drawn a crude outline of a female form, to which someone had later added a face, with finer brushstrokes.

"Pullman started off as a master carpenter. But he made his first fortune by keeping houses on swampy ter-rain from subsiding. Don't ask me how he did it."

"Can you imagine the way this must have been once, when it was full of workers and noise and productivity?"

"There's nothing but rats and mice here now," said Louise. "Watch yourself, everything's filthy."

Once, she took my hand as we were walking over an uneven bit of ground, where clumps of grass had shot up.

"Come on, I'll show you the archive," she said. "I can't spend all day giving you a tour of the place."

As expected, the archive wasn't terribly helpful to me. There was hardly anything to do with the early history of

the company. A lot had been thrown away, Louise admitted, and some things had been given to the library.

"You wouldn't have found anything about the Pullman Strike here anyway," she said. "They didn't like to
talk about it then, and no one cares about it today."

She was leaning against a rack where dusty cardboard
boxes were stacked. The archive was right at the top of
the building, and the air here was warm and dry. The only
light came from above, through Plexiglas skylights. Neither of us said anything. Louise looked at me and smiled.
I kissed her.

"You don't love me, and I don't love you. But what's it
matter," she said, laughing. "So long as we're having fun."

# 24

I didn't think about Agnes while I was with Louise, and I was fine. When I came home, I felt like I was going back to prison. I left the apartment door ajar, but then I heard voices outside in the corridor, and I went to shut it. I lay down on the sofa for half an hour, then I got up and went to the library, and from there on to the lake, to the café at the end of Grant Park.

I was thinking about the baby Agnes was carrying. I wondered if it would be like me, or have a character like mine. I couldn't imagine what it would feel like if there was a child of mine somewhere in the world. Even if I never saw Agnes again, I would still be a father. It will change my life, I thought, even if I never get to see it. And then I thought, I couldn't stand never to see it. I want to know what kind of kid it is, what it looks like. I got out my notebook and tried to sketch a face. I couldn't do it, so I started writing instead:

*Our baby was born on May 4. It was a little girl. She was very small and light and had very fine blond hair. We called her . . .*

For a long time I thought about what I was going to call the baby. The waitress brought me a refill, and I saw she had a nametag with "Margaret" on it. I thanked her for the coffee and wrote:

*. . . Margaret. We put her crib in my study. Every night she cried, and every day we took her for walks in her stroller. We would stop in front of the toyshop and wonder what to buy her, later, when she was older. Agnes said she didn't just want Margaret to have dolls.*

*"I want her to play with cars and airplanes and computers and trains."*

*"Yes, but we're starting her off with cuddly toys and dolls . . ." I said.*

*"Legos," said Agnes. "When I was little, I used to like Legos much better than dolls. I think Margaret should have whatever she wants."*

*"I can teach her all about luxury trains, if you like," I said.*

*We started looking for a more spacious apartment, on the edge of town somewhere, where there were parks and woods. We thought about moving to California or Switzerland. My book was going well, in spite of the extra work with the baby. It was the happiest summer of my life, and Agnes too had rarely been so happy.*

That's all I wrote. I realized I knew precious little about babies, and decided to get a book on the subject. I was convinced now that Agnes and I would get together again. I wrote a letter to her, stuffed it in my pocket, and went home as fast as I could.

I was just opening the front door of the apartment when I heard the phone ringing. I picked it up, still in my coat. It was a colleague of Agnes's, one of the violinists in her quartet.

"I've been trying to get hold of you all day," she said.

"I've been out walking," I said.

She hesitated.

"Agnes is sick," she finally said, "she hasn't been coming to rehearsal."

"What are you playing?" I asked, I have no idea why.

"Schubert," she said. Then for a moment she said nothing.

"Agnes would kill me, if she knew I got in touch with you. But I think she needs your help."

"What's the matter with her?" I asked, but that was all she was prepared to say.

"I think you should go and see her," she said, "she's not well."

I thanked her and promised to visit Agnes. I tore up the letter I'd written. I got a beer out of the fridge and sat down by the window.

If I go and see Agnes now, I thought, that'll be it forever. It's hard to explain; although I loved her and had been happy with her, it was only when she wasn't there that I felt I was free. And my freedom had always mattered more to me than my happiness. Maybe that was what my girlfriends meant when they talked about my egoism.

I didn't go to see Agnes that day or the next. On the third day, I decided to go. Exceptionally, I took a taxi, so as not to lose even more time. I asked the driver to stop outside a bookstore, and ran in and asked for a book about babies. The sales assistant recommended one with the title *How to Survive the First Two Years*.

# 25

Agnes came to the door in her robe. She was very pale. She asked me in, and I followed her into the room. She lay down again. I sat by her for a while, not saying anything, then I asked: "Are you not well?"

"I lost the baby," she said quietly.

I'd never thought of the possibility of miscarriage. I felt relieved and ashamed at the same time.

Agnes smiled and said: "You ought to be pleased, really." But cynicism wasn't her style.

"It's not your fault," she said, "the doctor says there's one miscarriage for every birth."

"Can you not have babies, then?" I asked.

"Yes, I can," she said, "but I need to take hormones if I get pregnant again."

"I'm sorry," I said.

She sat up and put her arms around me.

"I missed you," she said. Then she began to cry. "It was six centimeters, the doctor said."

"When did it happen?"

"I was in the hospital for three days," said Agnes. "They had to perform a curettage. The doctor kept talking about the embryonic matter. So I don't get infected. It wasn't viable. The embryonic matter."

I stayed with Agnes overnight, lying fully clothed next to her on the mattress, unable to sleep. I got up very early. I felt like reading something, but there was only the *Norton Anthology of Poetry* and a few manuals. There was a collection of clipped coupons for ten-cent reductions off the price of a jar of peanut butter or a box of cereal. I went to get a glass of orange juice. The kitchen was squeaky clean, as though it had never been used for anything. The fridge was almost empty. I looked in the cupboards. Among the cleaning things was a pair of rubber gloves, marked "Kitchen" in black felt-tip. Out of curiosity, I looked in the bathroom, and found the corresponding pair duly marked "Bathroom." There was a pile of colorful cleaning cloths next to them. One of them was old and faded, and someone had stitched "Agnes" on it. I went back to the living area. From the corner that had the mattress in it, I could hear Agnes stirring, and muttering something to herself. I sat down at her desk and pulled open a drawer. There was an old carton full of letters and postcards, carefully arranged by sender. There were little index cards, marked "Parents," "Grandparents," "Uncles/Aunts," "Cindy," and "Herbert." There was a file card with my name on it too, but the section behind it was empty. I had once sent Agnes a pretty bland postcard from New York, but that was in the kitchen taped to the fridge. I pulled the batch of Herbert's letters out of the box. First, there were some postcards, then letters, then more postcards, and finally three new letters, the last of which was very thick and only recently postmarked Chicago. I peered into the envelope, without taking out the letter, and read "Dear Agnes." I put the letters back in the box, and sat on a chair by the window. I must have fallen asleep at some point.

In the morning, Agnes was feeling a bit better, and she got up for breakfast.

"I didn't really mean that, you know," I said. "I thought about it for a long time. I tried to reach you."

"It wasn't what you said. It was the fact of your leaving me on my own. The way you just ran off."

"If you want a baby . . ."

"You don't really want one. But that doesn't matter anymore now."

"Maybe later," I said.

"Sure," said Agnes, "maybe later."

# 26

Agnes moved back in with me. She was more affected by the miscarriage than I first thought. We didn't talk about it when we were together, but she often sat alone in the bedroom, looking out of the window. In among all the buildings, you could just make out a tiny patch of lake.

"What do the birds do when the lake's frozen over?" Agnes asked once.

"I don't think it ever freezes completely," I said, "and if it does, the animal-welfare people make holes in the ice, or they feed the birds or something. I don't really know."

Agnes hadn't gone back to her studies yet. Her professor had said she might stay home till Christmas. He seemed to have a very high opinion of her, and when she talked about him, I almost felt jealous.

"He's an old man," she said.

"So am I. I'm an old man too."

"He's twice your age."

I told Agnes about Louise. She didn't say anything, she didn't even get angry. Her indifference offended me.

"Write it down," she said, "carry on with the story, and write down everything that's happened. The baby, the lake, Louise..."

"I have gone on with it," I said, "in the story you've had the child."

I was reluctant to show Agnes what I'd written. But she asked to see it, and when she'd read it she was pleased. Her only objection was to the name I'd chosen.

"What would you like to call it, then?"

"It's already been given a name. You can't change it now."

"I bought a book," I said.

"Tell me about Margaret," said Agnes, "if she's born on the fourth of May, that makes her a ... What's the sign?"

"A Taurus. I thought you didn't believe in astrology."

"That doesn't matter. You've got that book about star signs, haven't you."

I got the book out, and read: "The Taurus character is defined by Venus. It is in this phase that spring has finally prevailed, something that manifests itself in the Taurus. Tauruses are peaceful and even-tempered, they need plenty of affection, and are capable of great passion."

Agnes took the book out of my hands, and started leafing through it.

"Here," she said. "They have excellent deductive powers and a logical brain. This often takes the form of an aptitude for mathematics. You see, she takes after me."

I looked over her shoulder. "The sign's proverb is 'Out of sight, out of mind.'"

"You must write it down," said Agnes, "you must give us our baby. I wasn't able to do it."

I sat at the computer all afternoon, and Agnes sat next to me, dictating or correcting. Our baby grew fast, within half a page it could walk, and a couple of sentences later, talk as well. We wrote about a visit to its grandparents in Florida, vacations in Switzerland, childhood diseases, and Christmas. Margaret was given beautiful presents. A tricycle, building blocks, dolls, her first book. Agnes and I got married, we had another child, a boy this time. We were happy.

"I can't do any more," I said at last, "we can't write a whole family epic in an afternoon."

"Then we'll go for a walk and think about what happens next," said Agnes.

# 27

We went out. Lately we'd been walking in the park, but now Agnes wanted to go into town. It was Saturday, and the streets were crawling with people doing their Christmas shopping. Agnes stopped in front of a toyshop.

"I want to buy a teddy bear for Margaret," she said. We went into the shop, and bought a big teddy bear.

Then Agnes said our baby should get a present from me as well, and we bought her a doll.

"Now let's go in the baby clothes section," said Agnes.

"Don't you think . . ." I hesitated. "Are you sure that's a good idea?"

But Agnes had already gone on ahead. When I caught up with her, I saw there were tears streaming down her face. Almost randomly, she picked up a few baby things as she went, a woolly sweater, a pair of striped dungarees, a bonnet. I tried to calm her down, but she wouldn't listen, paid with her credit card, and ran out of the shop. I set off after her, but almost lost her as she weaved her way through the great crowds. I only caught up with her by the Doral Plaza. She was walking more slowly now, though she still wouldn't speak. Neither of us saying anything, we rode the elevator up. Once in the apartment, Agnes put down her shopping bags, and went into the bedroom.

I was just taking my shoes off when she raced past me into the bathroom, and slammed the door and locked it. I could hear her wailing loudly.

"What's the matter?" I called through the door.

"In the bedroom . . ." she sobbed.

I went into the bedroom. There was a suspended platform outside the window, with a couple of men on it who were cleaning the windows. They finished, waved to me, and floated back up. I'd had a note from the management announcing that the windows were going to be cleaned, but I'd forgotten to mention it to Agnes. I lowered the blinds, and went out into the corridor. In the bathroom I could still hear Agnes whimpering. I knocked, and finally she opened.

"They were looking at me," she said, wiping away her tears with toilet paper, and blowing her nose.

"They've gone now. I've drawn the blinds too."

"They were looking at me. They were all looking at me when we were buying the things for the baby. They all know it's a lie."

"But it's just a story. You wanted me to—"

"I didn't know . . ." Agnes interrupted me, and that was all she said.

"You wanted me to write that way," I said, "we wrote it together."

"I didn't know it was going to be so real. But it's still a lie. It's sick."

"I thought it might help you. It helped me while you were gone."

"It's not true. You have to write it the way it was and the way it is. You have to be truthful."

"Yes," I said.

"Write what happens next," said Agnes. "We have to know what will happen next."

"OK. I'll write what we do, where we go, what you wear. Like before. You can wear your navy dress again. When it gets a bit warmer."

"I'll put it on tonight."

That very evening, Agnes threw all our newly bought baby things down the garbage chute in the corridor. I was in favor of giving them away, but Agnes insisted on getting rid of them. When the teddy bear didn't fit in the small opening, she tore the arms off it. Also, we deleted what we'd written on the computer that afternoon. And then Agnes put on the navy dress.

"When I was little, my best friends were the characters in the books I read," she said, "my only friends, in fact. It was like that later too. After I finished *Siddhartha*, I stood in the garden for an hour to mortify my flesh. The only flesh I succeeded in mortifying was in my feet. There was snow in the garden."

Agnes laughed hesitantly. I'd put a frozen pizza in the oven, and was opening a bottle of wine. "I'm always sad, each time I finish a book," said Agnes. "It feels to me as though I've become the character in it, and the character's life ends when the books does. I suppose there are times I'm glad too. Then the ending is like coming out of a bad dream, and I feel all light and free, reborn. I some-times wonder whether writers really know what they're doing to us readers."

I kissed Agnes.

"So here I am sitting with you, and I didn't even know your head was full of the entire cast list of world literature."

"I don't read much anymore," said Agnes, "maybe for that reason. Because I didn't want books to have me in their power. It's like poison. I imagined I'd become immune. But you never become immune. On the contrary."

Then we ate, and afterward Agnes took the sedative the doctor had prescribed after her operation. I sat on the side of the bed, waiting for her to go to sleep.

"Now we're together again," she mumbled, "just the two of us."

# 28

Agnes slowly seemed to get better. But it was as though she'd removed herself from me, and couldn't find our old intimacy again. When we went for a stroll, she would walk beside me completely self-involved; when I held her hand, she quickly freed herself again. She read the *Norton Anthology* a lot. When I was out, she often played her cello. I could hear it from the corridor, but as soon as I opened the door, she would stop.

"Would you play something for me?" I asked her once. She just said: "No."

While she was putting her cello in its case, I leafed through her sheet music.

"I thought you were playing Schubert?"

"Not anymore," said Agnes with a smile, "the others thought that wasn't what I needed just now, and so we're playing Mozart."

"I don't like Mozart."

"I don't either."

It was Advent. There was the first snow of the year. Agnes had decorated the apartment with white stars that she'd woven from strips of paper. I had given her a tape of carols that she listened to the whole time, even though she thought the music was horrible, and only a European would find favor in something that kitschy. When I got home from the library in the evening, she would kiss me quickly on the lips. She would often light candles. She said she was thinking about her childhood a lot, but she didn't go into any detail. She asked me about what people did at Christmas in Switzerland. We baked some cookies, which didn't really taste right, because we didn't have all the spices, and I made Agnes an Advent wreath out of newspaper and fir twigs.

"Even though it's too late really," I said.

"That doesn't matter," she said.

In bed, Agnes often turned her back on me, and slept curled up in a ball on her side. When she had a shower, she would lock the door and get changed in the bathroom, just as she had during our first few weeks together. I thought all that was temporary and we would soon be back to normal.

Agnes was busy in a way she hadn't been previously. She got plenty of exercise, went swimming, and joined a gym. She attended rehearsals of the quartet, visited her colleagues at the university, and brought work home with her. She'd gotten some new slides of crystal lattices, and sat at the window, holding them up to the light.

"People have known for a long time that that's how they look. Long before it could be proved. Theoretically, you can take any crystal—except the tricline-asymmetrical ones—and turn it over and fit it in the same space."

"Explain them to me," I asked.

"They're created by the interaction of atoms and molecules. Every little bit has its own fixed place in relation to the others. But perfect crystals are very rare in nature. There are almost always irregularities and malformations."

Once Agnes came out to the lake with me, and we brought stale bread to feed the birds. When the shops had closed, we walked back through the downtown area, and looked in the shop windows. I was worried that the baby things we would see would disturb Agnes, but she remained calm. When I asked, she said: "I can have a baby any time I want."

"Do you want one?"

"Maybe. Sometime."

When we got back, Agnes said: "We have to clean the apartment. Everything needs to be spotless for Christmas."

"We're not expecting anyone."

"That doesn't matter. We'll clean it for ourselves. You didn't do anything while I was away."

We spent the whole evening cleaning.

"You've got even fewer things than I do," said Agnes, once we were finished.

"Yes, but this is only a part of it. Most of it's in Switzerland. Furniture, clothes, and especially books."

"I keep forgetting you're only a visitor."

"I could stay. Or you could go back with me."

"Yes. Maybe. A happy ending for your story."

"For our story, you mean."

# 29

We celebrated Christmas Eve together. It was some time since I'd last shown Agnes what I'd written. Now I printed out the story on white paper and put it in a folder with a dedication.

"I haven't got an ending yet," I said, "but as soon as I do, I'll have the whole thing bound into a little book for you."

Agnes had knitted me a sweater.

"God knows, I had enough wool," she said.

"Black wool?"

"No, I had it dyed. Light blue doesn't really suit you."

I didn't say anything. We were sitting on the sofa, with a little Christmas tree in front of us, that Agnes had decorated only with candles. From next door we could hear the sound of Christmas carols and squabbling children, then a loud, low voice shouting something. And then silence.

"I'm sorry," I said, "I wasn't thinking of that."

"This morning there was a parcel for you from UPS. I thought it was probably a present, so I didn't mention it."

I recognized the handwriting right away.

"It's from Louise."

"Open it."

Inside it was the model of a Pullman lounge car. It was beautiful and perfect. Behind the windows you could see little figures sitting at tables.

"Here's a card too," said Agnes, "it's an invitation to her New Year's party."

The card was from Louise's parents. It was a printed invitation, only my name had been written in by hand. On the back, Louise had written: "Come if you can. Bring Agnes with you, if you like. Lots of interesting people!"

"Did you tell her about me?" asked Agnes.

"Only that you'd left me, and then that you came back."

"*You* left *me*, I think you mean. And then you came back to me."

"Christmas is a depressing time, if you think about it," I said.

"Children enjoy it."

"Come on," I said, "let's go up on the roof."

It was freezing up on the roof. The gale almost took our breath away, and we tried to shelter behind the little construction that housed the elevator machinery. This time we did see stars, masses of stars, it looked like the sky was made of nothing but stars. I saw the Milky Way, and Agnes pointed out Orion and Gemini.

"I didn't know you knew about stars," I said.

"What do you know about me anyway," said Agnes, but it didn't sound bitter.

She leaned against me, and I kissed her hair. We stood on the roof for a long time, looking up at the sky, neither of us saying anything. Then we heard a siren going off down below, and, in spite of the wind, we went over to the guardrail and looked down. We saw an ambulance, soon followed by a police car.

"Something's happened," said Agnes.

"Sometimes I try and imagine what it would be like to be someone else, like the ambulance driver for example," I said. "What would things look like to me then."

"Whenever something happens like on Christmas Eve, you can't help thinking it's particularly awful. As though the date mattered."

"We imagine we all share the same world. But each of us is in a mine or quarry of his own, just chipping away at his own life, doesn't look left or right, and can't even turn back because of the rubble he leaves behind him."

"Come on, let's go inside. I'm cold."

When we were back in the apartment, we both felt chilled to the bone. I ran a bath. Agnes walked into the bathroom. She got undressed and got in the bath with me. She sat with her back to me, and I put my arms around her. I washed her back, then we changed places, and she washed mine. We stayed in the bath for a long time, and kept adding more hot water. Then we dried each other, and I rubbed and combed Agnes's hair. Agnes turned the light out in the bedroom, and we made love.

"That was a present," she said afterward, as we lay side by side on the bed.

"What do you mean?"

"It's Christmas."

"I don't want you to sleep with me if you don't want to."

"But it was a present."

"Thank you very much," I said, and turned away.

Agnes didn't say anything.

"Do you ever see Louise?" she asked after a while.

"Sometimes in the library. There's nothing I can do about it."

"Would you like to do something about it?"

"There's nothing between us anymore."

"And what used to be between you?"

"Nothing," I said. "I told her you'd come back."

"*You* came back."

"She knows lots of stuff about Pullman, and she can introduce me to interesting people."

"How wonderful."

"Yes."

"Did you sleep with her?" asked Agnes.

"Does it matter?"

"Yes."

"What about you and Herbert?"

"No."

"Why would you have gone to him with the baby?"

"Because he's there for me. Because he loves me."

"So why did you come back to me?"

"Well, if you don't know that..." said Agnes. "Because I love you, and only you. Even if you won't believe it."

# 30

The next day, Agnes had a cold.

"Being up on the roof is bad for you," I said.

She stayed in bed all day, and read, while I sat in the living room, watching television. I went out briefly in the afternoon, to buy bread. I'd been boycotting the store by the entrance for several weeks. It was snowing hard, and the wind blew it right in my face. When I got back to the apartment, Agnes was sitting in bed, cross-legged. The blanket had slipped off her knees. She was crying.

"You should keep yourself covered," I said. "What's the matter?"

The *Norton Anthology* lay open in her lap, and she pointed to a poem. "A Refusal to Mourn the Death, by Fire, of a Child in London," by Dylan Thomas.

*Deep with the first dead lies London's daughter,*
*Robed in the long friends,*
*The grains beyond age, the dark veins of her mother,*
*Secret by the unmourning water*
*Of the riding Thames.*
*After the first death, there is no other.*

"I don't get it," I said.

"If there's no more death, there's no more life either," said Agnes.

"It's only a poem," I said, "you shouldn't take it so seriously. It's just words."

"A child has died in me," said Agnes, "in my belly, it was six centimeters already. I couldn't save it. It grew inside me, and then it died inside me. Do you know what that means?"

"Are you still thinking about that?" I said.

Agnes turned away and cried into her pillow. The book fell to the ground. I picked it up and pulled up the blankets. She slept into the late afternoon, and I read. When she woke up, she was calmer. But she had a temperature, and her cold had gotten worse. I made her some tea, and sat with her until she was asleep again. Then I went for a walk by the lake.

The snow had stopped. When I was really cold, I went to the café at the end of the park. The waitress switched on the light, and brought me a coffee. Then she disappeared again through the door behind the bar. I looked out over the lake. For the first time, I thought about our baby, not just about Agnes, and her pregnancy, and her loss. Not about Margaret either. I thought about the baby, which was six centimeters, which I had never known and never wanted, and which was now lost. It didn't have a name and it didn't have a face. I didn't even know if it had been a boy or girl. I had never asked Agnes about that. I walked out of the café. It had gotten dark by now, and while I walked along the shore, my thoughts ordered themselves, and suddenly I knew how Agnes's story would continue. It was as though a door had opened, and I could see it all clearly, and it was all within reach. Agnes was still asleep when I got back. I shut the bedroom door, and sat down at the computer. I felt quite numb, maybe because I'd come in from the cold, and because the apartment was so warm, too warm. I'd gotten almost as far as Christmas in the story, but I took up the story after the holidays. I sensed right away that Agnes was closer to me than usual. It was as though it wasn't me writing—I was just describing a film that was showing inside my head. I saw Agnes standing on an empty train platform. It was nighttime. A train drew up, almost empty, and Agnes boarded it. I wrote.

*The journey to Willow Springs took the best part of an hour. By the time Agnes got out, it was well past midnight, but you could still hear the rockets going off, and sometimes the whole sky was bright with fireworks. Agnes was cold, in spite of her winter coat, but even being cold seemed to be at a remove from her, it was as though she knew she was cold, without feeling it. She walked down long streets, past rows of small wooden houses, some of them still echoing with music and the sound of people talking and laughing...*

It felt as though I was writing quickly, but it was actually quite late when I couldn't do any more, when the pictures froze and lost their resolution. I read over what I'd written, and it felt as though I was reading it for the first time. I didn't know where this was going, but I knew I couldn't go on like that, it was impossible for Agnes and unbearable for me, I needed to find an ending, a good ending, for Agnes's sake. But I felt too tired; I saved what I'd written, and switched off the computer.

I got undressed and lay down next to Agnes. She was breathing deeply and evenly, and without waking, turned to me and put her arm around my waist. I fell asleep instantly.

# 31

"Did you write the ending?" Agnes asked me the next morning. She was feeling better, but her voice sounded hoarse, and it hurt when she swallowed.

"I'm not finished yet," I said.

Agnes got up for breakfast, but had to go straight back to bed afterward. Her mother called. I picked up the receiver. I had never spoken to Agnes's parents, or even given them any thought. Apart from the odd phone call, Agnes seemed not to have much contact with them.

I brought the telephone into the bedroom. Back in the living room, I could hear Agnes say: "A friend who's just dropped by. I've got a bit of a cold." After she hung up, I went in to see her.

"Don't your parents know about me, then?" I asked.

"Were you listening to my conversation?"

"I just heard you say something about a friend drop-ping by."

"I don't tell them much about what I'm up to. I don't think they're all that interested. They'd only worry."

"Why, because of me?"

"Because of everything. They barely know the first thing about me."

"Is that because they're living down in Florida?"

"My mother wanted to stay here with me, but my father . . . I told them I wouldn't visit them. I've never been to see them down there."

"You're tough."

"I thought it was tough for me when they left. Now I don't need them anymore, and they don't need me yet. I'm sure I'll be hearing from them . . ."

"How do they know my number?"

"I had my calls rerouted."

There had never been a call for Agnes before. I went back to my study. I had decided to forget what I wrote yesterday, and write a new ending. But I didn't delete the text, I saved it in a file I called "Ending 2." I felt a sense of relief as soon as I started writing. I thought I could make up for what I'd done wrong yesterday. I wrote more consciously than usual, and faster; I knew what I wanted, and I chose the shortest way that would get me there.

I described the holidays exactly as they had been, only without the feeling of distance between Agnes and me, without her tears and Louise's present. I wrote about a wonderful week between Christmas and New Year's, how we cooked together, and went for walks, all bundled up in our warmest clothes, through Grant Park in the snow, and to the Adler Planetarium, where Agnes explained the stars to me, and to the library, where we looked up old Christmas stories.

*Agnes was back with me. We knew now that we belonged together, and that knowledge helped her overcome the loss of the baby. Just as the baby had once sundered us, now its loss brought us together. Sorrow and pain bound us closer together than happiness ever had.*

*We celebrated New Year's at home. We didn't go up on the roof, because Agnes still had a cold. We sat by the window, and watched the snow.*

I heard the cello playing in the bedroom. Normally, the slightest noise is enough to put me off when I'm writing, but now I welcomed the distraction. I wrote almost without thinking, though it wasn't the same as the state of unconscious concentration I'd been in yesterday.

*We'd turned on the television to watch the live broadcast of the New Year's festivities from Times Square in New York. Tens of thousands of people had gathered there, and were gazing up at the enormous artificial apple that was slowly being lowered toward them. At midnight on the dot, it touched the ground. The crowds cheered, people screamed and hugged each other. Somewhere singing began; the singing seemed to grow from the noise, which gradually faded, till there was nothing to be heard but the old song.*

*Should auld acquaintance be forgot*
*And never brought to mind?*

*In Chicago it was only eleven o'clock, but Agnes and I stood up. We embraced and toasted our future, while in New York people continued to sing:*

*But seas between us broad have roar'd,*
*Sin' auld lang syne.*
*For auld lang syne, my jo,*
*For auld lang syne,*
*We'll take a kiss o' kindness yet*
*For auld lang syne.*

Agnes had stopped playing, and had come into the study.

"I don't want you to finish the story," she said.

"Why not?"

"It's not good. We don't need it."

"But I have finished it."

"Really?" she said. She hesitated. "Does it end happily?"

"Of course it does. In America, all stories end happily."

Agnes smiled. "Will you read it to me?" she asked.

"You go to bed," I said.

# 32

I'm not very good at reading aloud. But that wasn't why Agnes was disappointed. She didn't say anything, and nor did I as I sat on the bed next to her.

"Are you happy with it?" I asked.

"Are *you* happy with it?"

"I'm not sure," I said. I wasn't convinced by the ending. It hadn't really come off, it wasn't alive, it wasn't real. I had written it the way I had wanted it to be. It was like a New Year's resolution that doesn't survive for more than a few hours before you disregard it, a well-intentioned but empty form of words.

"Endings are always difficult," I said. "Life doesn't go in for endings, it goes on."

"It's a present, then," said Agnes. "A New Year's present."

She tried to look me in the eye, and I put my arms around her so as not to look back at her, and I said: "I'll put it in a folder along with the other pages, and then you'll have your little book. A book called *Agnes*."

When Agnes came out of the bedroom a little later, I

hadn't yet begun on that. I was sitting in the wicker chair, staring out at the falling snow.

"What are you doing?" she asked.

"Thinking."

"About the story?"

"Yes," I said. The film in my head had started up again.

Over the next few days, I was restless. Agnes seemed to have caught it from me, and she wasn't well either, and her cold had gotten worse too. She said her throat hurt each time she swallowed, she suffered blinding headaches, and she stayed in the bedroom almost all the time.

I had made up a little booklet of all my pages plus the ending. But as soon as Agnes was asleep, I went back to work on the story. I went over the whole thing, and replaced the ending with "Ending 2," which, as I'd already sensed, had been coming all along. It was the only logical, and the only true ending for the story.

When Agnes asked me what I was working on, I said I was back on the luxury trains. I was often absent-minded with her, I would rather have been writing the whole time. It was as though I was living the story now, as though everything else was insignificant and unreal, and as though eating and sleeping were just a waste of time.

I was irked with Agnes for being ill. I still made her cups of tea and brought her her meals in bed, but she couldn't help feeling my impatience and being hurt by it.

"You don't have to hang around here all day just to look after me," she said. "Go to the library if you want. Maybe you'll meet Louise."

"That's not the point. I'm just sorry you're spending your holidays like this. I hate sitting around at home all day."

"There's no reason why you should. I'm not on my deathbed yet. I'm perfectly OK, as long as I can stay in bed."

I walked over to the lake again, and strolled through Grant Park. When it got to be too cold for me, I went to the library. Louise wasn't there. I got myself a novel, and read it for an hour or so. Then I put it back, without bothering to find out what happened at the end.

"You were gone a long time," said Agnes on my return.

"But you said you wanted to be on your own."

"I wasn't complaining, don't be so touchy. I said I didn't mind if you went out for a bit. I never said I wanted to be on my own."

"Did you sleep?"

"No, I watched television."

"I thought you had to stay in bed?"

"I was covered up."

I cooked something, and we ate in the kitchen.

"What shall we do for New Year's Eve?" I asked.

"I don't think I'll be better by then."

"How do you know? Don't you want to go out somewhere with me?"

"No, I'd like to. But I'm not well. I don't feel well. Did you go to the library?"

"Yes, but not on account of Louise. I was getting to feel cold, and I wasn't ready to come home. I didn't want to bother you."

"You don't bother me. I was just saying you don't have to spend all day looking after me. It's fine if you go out. It's fine if you want to go to Louise's party."

"Really?"

"Yes, really."

"She knows lots of interesting people. It might even be useful for the book."

"We're not married or anything."

"It might be useful for us too. If I'm to stay in this country, I need to meet some of the right people."

"I don't want to argue with you," said Agnes, "I'm tired and I don't feel well."

# 33

"Your hair's getting thin," said Agnes, "you're getting old."

I'd gone into the bedroom to say goodbye.

"Will you promise me to take a taxi back," she said.

"I might be very late. You're not to worry about me."

"Will you call me at midnight?"

"I can't promise you. You know what it's like at a New Year's party at midnight. But I'll try."

We embraced, and she kissed me passionately.

"All the best," she said.

"Hey," I said, laughing, "I'll be back."

"I just meant if you don't call . . . Happy New Year."

I called Agnes just after eleven o'clock.

"You're far too early," she said.

"I thought I might forget later. What are you up to?"

"I'm having something to eat. I watched the celebrations in New York. The New Year's already started there."

"I know."

"I miss you."

"Go to bed. When you wake up, I'll be back."

Louise was standing next to me while I telephoned. She had an ironic smile on her face.

"Are you missing your little girlfriend?" she asked, when I'd hung up.

"She's sick."

"American girls are always sick, but it's never serious. They keep you in a state of permanent guilt about them. On the other hand, if they sleep with a guy, they talk about it afterward as though they'd done him a service. Like walking their dog or something. Because the dog needs walkies."

"Agnes isn't like that."

"Sure," said Louise. She linked arms with me, and introduced me to a few of her guests. She smiled and said a few words to each one, but as soon as we were alone again, she told me which of the men had come on to her, and who had deceived whom.

"Why are you living with your parents, if their world is so repulsive to you?" I asked.

"Oh, they're fine, they're not repulsive to me."

"But why don't you get an apartment of your own, and have your own friends over?"

"If it was up to me, I would have gone back to France long ago. But I've got a good job here. And I don't really mind where I'm living." Anyway, she said, her apartment had its own separate entrance, and she could come and go as she pleased.

"Then why didn't you ask any of your friends?"

"Why should I? Haven't I got you!"

"Do you have any friends over here?"

"I've always found men easier to get on with than

women. And I didn't want to ask more than one man at a time. After all, I've got a reputation to lose."

I drank quite a lot, and talked to Louise all night. Her mother winked at me a couple of times, and once her father came over and put his arm around me, and asked if I was having a good time. I thanked him for the invitation, and he said he was pleased I'd been able to come. He asked me what I'd managed to find out about the Pullman Strike. "I think the role of money in the whole dispute has been exaggerated," I said. "It was about freedom. Pullman was a patriarch, and the strike was a protest more against him and his absolute power in their lives, and not just against their exploitation."

"Revolutions are always about power. And power is money."

"But even without the Depression, the workers were on a collision course with him. Even if wages hadn't been lowered and prices raised."

"Believe me, young man, it was about money pure and simple," said Louise's father, taking his arm away. "You writers attach too much importance to ideas. I'm a businessman. I know what makes the world go round."

When I was alone with Louise again, she said: "You shouldn't discuss politics with my father. What do you care about that Pullman business anyway? That's all long buried and forgotten."

I said that what had happened then in that one model community was what was happening now all over the world, and that sooner or later there would be a similar reaction against it.

Louise made a disparaging gesture. "Come on, let's go up to my place," she said. "There won't be a revolution tonight. Everyone's too drunk for a start."

She got a bottle of champagne from the fridge, and I followed her up the wide staircase into her little apartment. She locked the door behind us.

# 34

It was three or four o'clock, and I was one of the last to leave. Louise insisted on taking me back.

"You'll never get a taxi at this time," she said.

It wasn't far to midtown. She pulled up on Beaubien Court, a little one-way street behind the Doral Plaza.

"I don't kiss my men on Michigan Avenue," she said.

"Agnes is back."

"You might have thought of that earlier."

"You don't love me."

"And she's stopped sleeping with you," said Louise, and she leaned across the automatic gears, and kissed me on the lips.

"She's sick," I said, "but she'll get better. There was something real and important between us. And it's not lost."

"You men are fools," said Louise, "you can only love in the face of rejection. Words, these big words the whole time. There was something between us too, tonight, and that was beautiful. And tomorrow night we could have it again, and a few more times in the nights to come. And maybe, if you were open to it, something might develop from that. But you were never up for it, right from the start. You always had me in a separate category."

"You told me you didn't love me. Back in the archive, remember?"

"I may have said it then, but I didn't say it tonight."

"I've got to go."

"Why? I'm in no hurry."

"I'm not a good man, Louise."

"You're just drunk."

"Yes. And now I've got to go. Thanks for the party. I'll call you."

"Say Happy New Year to your Cinderella from me," Louise said bitterly, and as I was walking up the back stairs to the building, she added: "Try bringing me one of her shoes sometime. You never know, it might fit me."

I couldn't open the front door of the apartment. I could get the key in, but I couldn't seem to turn it. I struggled with it for a few minutes. I didn't feel drunk anymore, but it was as though my thoughts had left my head, and were floating around me. I tried all the keys I had, even the key to my place in Switzerland, even my trunk key, which I carry everywhere with me. I had to win time. Then I thought Agnes had changed the lock while I was gone, or some drunken asshole had stuck something in it. Or maybe Agnes had left the key in the lock, either on purpose or by accident. I rang the bell. I waited a couple of minutes, then I rang a second time, and then a third. Finally the door opened a crack, as much as the chain would allow. A Japanese man in a white robe was looking at me in alarm. I immediately realized what I'd done.

"I think I must be on the wrong floor," I said, "I'm really sorry."

The Japanese man merely nodded, and shut the door.

I was on the floor below. I went up the stairs. The stairs had been built in case of an emergency, and they were always kept lit. I sat down on one of the steps. I could hear the elevator going by, and I wondered who was going up or down at this time, only a few yards away from me. In the whole year I'd been living in the Doral Plaza, I'd met none of my neighbors, only the guy who ran the shop at the bottom. And all I knew about him was that he always seemed to be in the shop, and that he was given to dirty jokes and innuendo. He always treated me as though we shared a secret, as though we'd been friends for years, and he winked at me and dropped hints I didn't understand. But in fact he was as much of a stranger to me as the people I sometimes saw in the foyer, and of whom I didn't even know whether they lived in the building or were just visiting someone. At last the commotion in the elevator shaft stopped, everything was quiet again, and I went on up the stairs.

# 35

The first thing I heard in the apartment was the hum from my computer. I walked into the study. The screen saver was on, with stars radiating out in all directions from some central point. If you kept your eye fixed on that point, you had the sensation of falling through space, as though you'd crashed through the glass and were being sucked into black infinitude. I'd often sat and stared at it for minutes on end, and Agnes had laughed at me and said it was just the illusion of space, in fact it was just a pattern of centrifugal lights expanding as they floated toward the edge of the screen, and not for nothing was it called "Starfield Simulation."

I pressed a key, and the end of my story appeared on screen. It was the new ending, the one I'd written secretly.

*For a long time, Agnes stared at the stars flying toward her on the screen. The mystery, she thought, is the void at the center. She felt herself being pulled ever deeper into it. It was as though she was diving into the screen, being converted into the words and sentences she had read there. The hand that switched off the computer wasn't her own, nor was the body that put on its clothing. Agnes left the apartment, took the elevator down, walked in a kind of trance past the doorman who had fallen asleep over his newspaper.*

*The journey to Willow Springs took the best part of an hour. By the time Agnes got out, it was well past midnight, but she could still hear the rockets going off, and sometimes the whole sky was bright with fireworks. Agnes was cold, in spite of her winter coat, but even being cold seemed to be at a remove from her, it was as though she knew she was cold, without feeling it. She walked down long streets, past rows of small wooden houses, some of them still echoing with music and the sound of people talking and laughing.*

*Agnes got to the end of the street. In front of her lay the park in utter darkness. She blindly took a few steps into the darkness, and then she was able to see again. It was as though she had entered another world. The sky that, tainted by the streetlights, had been like an orange blanket over the suburb was of a transparent blackness here. She could see innumerable stars, and she could make out Orion and Gemini. The crescent moon was so new that she could barely pick out the snow-covered paths by its light.*

*The wind was stormy. The gusting in Agnes's ears was loud enough to drown every sound, every thought. She lost her way on the tangling paths, and it took her a long time to find the place in the forest again. The trees had lost their leaves, and the lake was frozen over. But Agnes recognized it. She pulled her gloves off, and ran her hands over the icy tree trunks. She didn't feel their cold, but their roughness on her almost numbed fingertips. Then she knelt down, and lay facedown in the powdery snow. Slowly she regained her feeling, first in her feet, in her hands, and then in her arms and legs, and it spread through her shoulders and her belly to her heart, until it had gone through her whole body, and it felt to her as though she was glowing in the snow, and her heat would surely melt it.*

There was a plate with a half-eaten sandwich on it next to the computer. I went into the bedroom. Agnes wasn't there. Her coat wasn't hanging on its hook. Nothing else was missing.

# 36

Agnes didn't return. I waited for her all night and all the following day. It stopped snowing at about noon, but it started again a few hours later. Once the telephone rang. I didn't pick it up, and it stopped before the answering machine clicked on.

I turned the light off, and put on the video that Agnes took of the time we hiked in the national park.

Me driving, on the way home, filmed from the backseat. The windshield wipers. Occasionally a car in front of us. The back of my head, my hands on the wheel. Finally I seem to have noticed that Agnes was filming. I turn my head and smile, but before I can turn all the way, the film stops.

PETER STAMM is the author of the novels *All Days Are Night*, *Seven Years*, *On a Day Like This*, and *Unformed Landscape*, and the short-story collections *We're Flying* and *In Strange Gardens and Other Stories*. His prize-winning books have been translated into more than thirty languages. For his entire body of work and his accomplishments in fiction, he was short-listed for the Man Booker International Prize in 2013, and in 2014 he won the prestigious Friedrich Hölderlin Prize. He lives in Switzerland.

MICHAEL HOFMANN has translated the work of Gottfried Benn, Hans Fallada, Franz Kafka, Joseph Roth, and many others. In 2012, he was awarded the Thornton Wilder Prize for Translation by the American Academy of Arts and Letters. His *Selected Poems* was published in 2009, and *Where Have You Been? Selected Essays* in 2014. He lives in Florida and London.

# ⚏ OTHER PRESS

*You might also enjoy these titles by Peter Stamm:*

## WE'RE FLYING

This short-story collection is a superb introduction to Peter Stamm's work and its precise rendering of the contemporary human psyche.

"These tautly constructed stories, with echoes of such disparate authors as Patricia Highsmith and Anton Chekhov, take root in the psyche and will not let you go." —*Library Journal*

## UNFORMED LANDSCAPE

A sensitive young woman is led to the richer life she was meant to have and is brave enough to claim. Her story speaks eloquently about solitude, the fragility of love, lost illusions, and self-discovery.

"Like the landscapes of his novels, Stamm's prose is spare and graceful." —*New Republic*

## ALL DAYS ARE NIGHT

In unadorned and haunting style, this novel forcefully tells the story of a woman who loses her life but must stay alive all the same.

"A postmodern riff on *The Magic Mountain* ... a page-turner." —*The Atlantic*

"Air[s] the psychological implications of our beauty obsession and the insidious ways in which it can obscure selfhood." —*New Republic*

"[An] engrossing story of recovery."
—*The New Yorker*

## SEVEN YEARS

**Torn between his highbrow marriage and his lowbrow affair, Alex is stuck within a spiraling threesome. *Seven Years* is a bold, sobering novel about the quest for love.**

"*Seven Years* is a novel to make you doubt your own dogma. What more can a novel do than that?"
—Zadie Smith, *Harper's Magazine*

## ON A DAY LIKE THIS

**On a day like any other, Andreas changes his life. Consumed with longing for his lost love and blinded by the uncertainty of his future, he is tormented by the question of what might have been.**

"What Peter Stamm has done with this novel is recreate life in all of its quiet banality — this is art — Stamm's achievement isn't the mere weaving of a story, it's the report of a life in quiet crisis."
—*Review of Contemporary Fiction*

## IN STRANGE GARDENS

**In this short-story collection, Stamm's clean style expresses despair without flash, through softness and small gestures.**

"With artful understatement, Stamm conveys the mutability of experience, a phenomenon as inscrutable as variations in the weather." —*Bookforum*

*And look for Peter Stamm's new novel,* To the Back of Beyond, *to be published in late 2017.*

*www.otherpress.com*